A Season of Surprises at the
Villa des Violettes
BOOK 2

Bestselling author of
the *Love in Provence* series

PATRICIA SANDS

PRAISE FOR THE FIRST NOËL AT THE VILLA DES VIOLETTES

BOOK 1 IN THE VILLA DES VIOLETTES SERIES

"...the best kind of escapist fiction—a delightful story with a gorgeous south of France setting."

"Charming characters and delightful food and wine imagery. Would love to visit the Villa des Violettes."

"I just took the most wonderful virtual Christmas holiday to the south of France in the pages of this book. Philippe and Kat are such wonderful characters and "spending" *The First Noël at the Villes des Violettes* is an adventure."

"*The First Noël at the Villa des Violettes* is filled with interesting characters, beautiful scenery, delicious foods, wonderful traditions, friendships, and lots of love. I loved every minute of it!"

"Patricia is a wonderful storyteller making you feel like you are in the South of France. The descriptions of the markets and the food had me salivating! The story has mystery, romance, friendships and celebrations. *The First Noël* was a wonderful read!"

A SEASON OF SURPRISES AT THE VILLA DES VIOLETTES

BOOK 2

PATRICIA SANDS

Cover art by Clare Strohman and Donna Fedele

ALSO BY PATRICIA SANDS

"The people of Provence greeted spring with uncharacteristic briskness, as if nature had given everyone an injection of sap."

— PETER MAYLE, *A YEAR IN PROVENCE*

*K*atherine wiped tears from her face with the back of her hand.

She reached for the box of tissues on the desk by her computer and then clicked on the next photograph. She could not stop laughing. Sometimes hooting out loud, she was editing photos, all taken at the annual New Year's Day swim in Antibes—the *bain du Jour de l'An*. Kat's camera, and many others, had captured priceless images as hundreds of people dashed into the frigid sea. She and Philippe were in several of them, wearing party hats and bathing suits.

The previous year, they had slept right through the Réveillon de la Sainte-Sylvestre, the New Year's Eve celebrations, and had gone to the beach the next day as spectators. This year, Philippe had persuaded her to take part.

"*C'est une grande tradition,*" he had assured her. Kat had known there was no way to get out of it.

Friends had joined them to splash in the sea, and these photos were proof of what an uproarious time it had been.

The weather had co-operated and, with both the water and the air at 17 degrees Celsius, the shock of the Mediterranean in winter had not been nearly as sharp as it could have been. Afterward, Philippe's long-time business partner, Gilles, invited their group back to his apartment for his customary New Year's Day "recovery" brunch, *la récupération*. Katherine thought it had been the best New Year's celebration ever. After all the angst she had suffered leading up to hosting her first Christmas/Fête de Noël in their restored villa, this had been relaxed and joyful. Now, weeks later, going through the photographs was bringing back all the happy memories. January was turning out to be a good month.

Kat had seen some of the photographs before, but many of those that were making her laugh were new to her. She had put out a call to friends and was now sorting through what they had sent for a few to post on the Instagram account she had opened as part of her promotion campaign for the Villa des Violettes' new bed and breakfast business.

Their first guests would arrive in a few weeks. They were starting off slowly with just one couple checking in first. Their hope was that the business would eventually provide some income.

"I can't believe how nervous I am about this," Kat had told Philippe when the first booking arrived.

Philippe had given her a reassuring hug. "Every new undertaking has its own challenges. It will be a whole new experience to welcome strangers into our home. *Un pas à la fois.*"

"One step at a time. I keep reminding myself about that. February tenth will be here before we know it. I'm glad we set that date. It gives us the opportunity to get everything ready for them and to enjoy the winter carnival in Nice before they get here."

It also was the amount of time Didier, their contractor

had said his crew needed to finish the new parking area. This work had been held up by the discovery in early autumn of Roman ruins where the parking area was originally going to go. Bureaucratic red tape had delayed work and had only been removed in December.

Now the ruins, which lay beside the driveway, were a focal point that added to the cachet of the property. Auguste, the keen gardener of Didier's crew, had helped Kat design plantings around it, and the look was beginning to take shape. With warmer weather on the way, Kat was excited about putting in a colorful border of annuals as a finishing touch.

Kat's emotions about starting this new business were a mixture of nervous trepidation and happy excitement. She vacillated between those feelings, but mostly in a good way. After what her friend Molly called her "Christmas conundrum," she was determined not to let anything drag her down again. Her goal now was to stay positive, no matter the challenges ahead. It was okay to feel anxious. She could deal with it.

Her work was interrupted now by the sound of Philippe's car, which she could see through the French doors coming up the gravel driveway. Rocco and Coco, the chocolate Labrador pups known together as Rococo, leaped up from where they had been sleeping by Kat's feet under the antique partners' desk and scrambled to the front door, where they barked a noisy greeting.

"*Coucouuuu, chérie!*" Philippe called.

"In the office, *mon chou!*" Kat answered back. "Come and join me for a good chuckle."

She lifted her face to Philippe as he leaned in to kiss her cheeks. The dogs bounced around him, demanding their fair share of his attention.

"How is your day going?" he asked.

"I've been busy here, except for a while this morning. I slipped out for a meeting with André at the gallery to talk about the spring exhibit."

André's well-established art gallery in Antibes had a large and loyal following. He had become her mentor after Philippe showed him some of Kat's work and had been enthusiastic about hanging a few of her photographs in the gallery. Now she felt a tingle of excitement as she recalled the first time a stranger purchased her work. She had almost burst with pride. Having her lifelong hobby—her passion— recognized and desired by others had been beyond her wildest dreams.

Philippe's eyes lit up. "*Ah oui.* The new show. The one last year went so well! What's the plan?"

Kat grinned and said that the meeting began with a glass of rosé. "I still haven't adjusted to wine in the morning."

"*Mais, c'est normal,*" Philippe said. "You know how we are at the *marché.*" There were few vendors' stalls that were without a bottle of rosé or pastis, a fresh baguette and slices of saucisson behind the counter each morning.

Barely containing her enthusiasm, Kat explained that André had invited her to show six of her latest photographs. "He asked if I also was interested in doing a series of shots from along the Mimosa Trail when the trees are in bloom. I missed seeing them flower last year when I was in Toronto. I can't wait to do this!"

"*Ah, la Route du Mimosa. Bonne idée.* But where exactly? It's a long trail, about 130 kilometres from one end to the other, starting around Grasse and ending at Bormes-les-Mimosas."

"André gave me a tip about a hiking path near Tanneron, where you can walk a long way under a canopy of mimosa trees. He described the explosion of the yellow blossoms and their scent in such poetic detail, he almost swooned. I want to take shots there," Kat said, barely pausing for breath. "He was only there once, many years ago, and has never gone back. For no good reason, he said. Have you been? Can you imagine?"

"I definitely can. I have often seen the mimosas in bloom, and you will see them around here, *bien sûr*, but not in such profusion as at Tanneron," Philippe said. "We have so many beautiful places to visit all around us, no one can possibly get to all of them. But I know you are going to give it a good try, *ma femme aventureuse*. You are always up for an adventure."

Their conversation halted while they watched Belle patter across the room with a kitten in her mouth.

"There she goes again," Kat exclaimed. "Moving house!"

The affectionate gray tabby had adopted Kat and Philippe in the autumn and then surprised them with her delicate condition. Now she was moving her offspring, one after another, under the skirt of an upholstered armchair next to the fireplace.

Belle had delivered six kittens on Epiphany, January 6, while Kat and Philippe and several friends were sitting around the dining table eating *Galette de Rois* and waiting to find out who would be crowned king.

Kat had prepared a box for Belle, which she had used for a while. She had proven to be a doting mother and Kat loved watching her nurture the babies the first few weeks. Now, not quite a month old, all six were on the verge of mobility, and for some mysterious reason, Belle had begun to move her brood every few days, one at a time, from one spot to another.

"We will simply give her the benefit of doubt," Kat said. "She must know what she's doing."

Philippe nodded. "And the dogs keep their distance, which amazes me. It's as if they know these kittens are fragile." He bent down and gave each of the dogs a rub. "These two must have loved splashing through the puddles this morning! Good thing you convinced me we needed a mudroom by the back door."

"How were things at the market today?" Kat asked

"*Très bien*. The regulars are getting back to their normal shopping habits now the holidays are over.

Life did seem to Kat to have settled into a tranquil rhythm, and she was glad there was no hint of any trouble on the horizon.

ebruary began with a reminder that not every day on the Côte d'Azur was idyllic. The first week was cool and rainy, and now a mistral had blown in to make things more miserable.

Philippe had the day off as the market was closed Mondays during the winter months. Katherine spent a quiet morning working on her photos before joining him in the kitchen, where he was preparing *croque monsieur* for lunch. Without planning it, this had become a weekly custom.

Kat had become a fan of the sandwich when she first arrived in France a year and a half earlier for the home exchange that changed her life. But it was the extra ingredient—that pinch of *herbes de provence* on the top layer of cheese—that Philippe added that made his version irresistible.

She prepared a salad of simple greens tossed with olive oil and lemon. And that was lunch.

"I'm concerned about some of the flooding in the hills north of Nice," Philippe said as he cleared the dishes. "From what I've seen online about conditions north of Entrevaux,

I'm not certain that Jacques will be able to deliver our weekly order of goat cheese. I'll give him a call this afternoon."

Kat stood at the window, her forehead wrinkled with worry. "Oh dear! I remember the floods last year. They caused such destruction. Let's hope it doesn't get that serious again. I must check with Véronique to see if she and David are up there now. But now, rain or no rain, I must take the dogs out."

She planned to take the dogs on a walk to visit Simone, their neighbor, whose grounds adjoined theirs, and went to put her rain jacket on.

"Do you think this weather will spoil Carnaval? Remember, we said we'd go on the weekend," Kat asked.

"*Non, Minou,*" Philippe replied. "*C'est normal.* We often have weather like this when Carnaval is on. I forgot you weren't here for it last year. It's not fun getting soaked, but people carry on with all the activities anyway."

"Because it's so beautiful here most of the time, I'm always surprised when we get a spell like this," Kat said. "I think in the past I've simply tried to ignore it. But taking out these fur babies of ours keeps it real."

The dogs, already soaking wet, came bounding to the back door when Kat called them. They had come a long way with their training in the past months and no longer needed to be leashed for the walk over to Simone's. When the weather was fine, Rococo were now able to spend a good part of the day outside in the large dog run Didier and his crew of Alfonso, Alesandro and Auguste had recently constructed for them off the mudroom.

"*Ah, chérie!* Now that the first day of guests is approaching, my excitement for you is mounting." Simone exclaimed as she led Katherine into her spotless kitchen. A sweet smell filled the room, a sure sign of her usual early morning baking session.

Kat had texted Simone to say she was on her way over, and so the tea was already steeping. She sat at the kitchen table with her dear friend to have a chat.

The previous summer, Kat had convinced Simone to buy a cell phone and use it to text messages. After living without such a convenience for her ninety-four years, Simone had resisted at first, but now admitted often that she found it helpful to be able to text. "You may convince me to embrace this new technology, after all," she would say from time to time, with a sparkle in her bright blue eyes.

Simone poured two cups of tea. "*Eh bien. Ainsi commence l'histoire,*" she said. "And so it begins. La Villa des Violettes will receive its first official guests in another week. I know Nicholas and Graham and his wife stayed with you for a few nights in August, but that doesn't count. That was just for fun, *oui*?"

"*Oui*! That was like having family stay," Kat said, smiling at the memory of their visit. "This will be different, *absolument.*"

They chatted about the places to visit that she could recommend to her first guests, and Kat admitted she was feeling a little jittery about their arrival.

Simone looked at her warmly and patted her arm. "*J'accepte la grande aventure d'être moi,*" she said. It was a Simone de Beauvoir quote that Simone had adopted as a mantra after the war, and which she had repeated often when Kat was struggling with some decisions the previous year.

Katherine's eyes lit up. "There's no question my life has

become an adventure. Sometimes I have to stop and pinch myself."

"There's nothing like a little pinch now and then to bring us back to reality," Simone said. Her voice dropped a tone. "By the way, have you heard from Delphine lately?"

"I haven't," Kat said. "Have you?"

"Since Christmas we have talked once or twice a week on the phone. I've become fond of her."

"Yes, it was so nice to see her feel comfortable with all of us at Christmas. It seems she's had a difficult childhood, and yet her sweet nature shines through. I'm glad you are forging a friendship with her."

"It works both ways, *chérie.* She brings a special something into my life, and I enjoy our conversations but ... " Simone fell silent

"But what?"

"Well, it's probably nothing. It's just that I haven't heard from her this week. I was concerned and called Monsieur Albert at the animal shelter to see if she was all right."

"And?"

"Well, you know how my intuition is. He said she had been under the weather and would be back at work soon. But it seems strange that she hasn't at least texted me.

Katherine was quiet for a moment, then she said, "Why don't I drive up and check on her. I've got time this afternoon."

Simone's eyes flickered with relief. "Merci! That's kind of you."

"Of course, we want to know she is okay. If she's sick I'll bring her back to our place."

"I would be happy to have her stay here, Kat."

"Let's see how she is first of all. I'll zip up there now."

Kat stood to put on her jacket and placed three apples

on the kitchen counter. "I've missed seeing Victor Hugo and the twins with this bad weather. I'm going to go out to the stable to give them all a big scratch and their treats before I go."

"*Bonne idée!* They will be happy to see you. And speaking of treats, there are yours. These are an advance tasting," Simone said, pointing to a plate heaped with the madeleines for which she was well known.

She had promised to bake these small, traditional French sponge cakes every day when guests were staying at the Villa des Violettes. Kat and Philippe had initially protested, but Simone said that baking them for their guests would let her feel involved in the bed and breakfast project. Kat was delighted at the prospect of serving them. Like Proust, she thought there was something evocative about their taste and shape. And Simone had a secret ingredient she refused to share.

She often quoted Proust's description of the little cake in his novel *Remembrance of Things Past*, "a little shell of cake, so generously sensual beneath the piety of its stern pleating."

"Thanks for these," Kat said, as Simone placed the little cakes in a paper bag. "They smell so good! I'm going to have to lock them away from Philippe."

"Enjoy those now, *chérie*, and share them with the boys." That was how she referred to Didier and his crew. "Alfonso told me he is going to pick them up each morning when you have guests. It is sweet how excited everyone is!"

"You are so right," Kat said. "Have you noticed how the whole crew has been pitching in to help Auguste revive the potager?"

While working on the restoration of the villa and stable, Auguste, whom Kat referred to affectionately as the gentle giant, had taken an interest in the gardens. He had cleared away the deadwood and other debris from the perennial beds that ran between the villa and the stone wall overlooking the sea. With Kat and Philippe's encouragement, he had shyly made suggestions about plantings that would give them flowers to cut all summer long.

When Kat had mentioned she would love to bring back to life the overgrown potager behind the kitchen, his eyes had sparkled. Together they had paced out a new layout. Then a few evenings later she had seen the crew at the potager site after their long work day was over. Two of them had power diggers and the other two had spades and were busy making the dream of a viable kitchen garden a reality.

"*Oui! C'était magnifique! Ils font des miracles!*" Simone said.

Kat smiled at Simone's mention of miracle workers. "You are right. They really are! It was splendid to see what they accomplished in such a short time. I've been working on the plans for planting, but you know I will consult with Auguste before we move to the next phase."

"Aha! *Le poulailler!*" Simone exclaimed.

Kat grinned. "Yes! The henhouse! Adorée has given us lots of advice. Who would have imagined that, in the last six months, our daughter, the investment banker in London, would turn into a village farmer in Sainte-Mathilde?"

Simone nodded. "*Incroyable!* What a transformation that has been. I can't wait to see her when she brings you the chicks. But now we must stop talking. Go to Mougins, and let me know as soon as you see Delphine. I want to stop worrying. You know that's not my normal state of mind."

Katherine gave Simone goodbye *bises*. "I will call you as soon as I see her and have found out what's happened. Hopefully it is nothing serious. There's a lot of flu going around."

ith the dogs settled in the back seat of her *deux-chevaux*, Kat was unhurriedly driving through the rolling hills north of Cannes on the scenic route to Mougins. She did think it was odd that Delphine had not been in touch with Simone, but she was not alarmed. She was sure the reason would be explained once she got there. When one of the hairpin turns gave her a panoramic view of the coast and the shimmering sea, happiness washed over her. *That is SO how I feel. I don't think I will ever stop having this response to the beauty of this part of the world.*

Traffic en route was light, and in less than a half hour she pulled into the parking lot of the animal shelter. Coco and Rocco popped up, instantly on the alert as they heard the dogs playing in the exercise yard.

"*Gentiment,*" Katherine cooed, giving each of them a treat. "Wait nicely. I won't be long."

Leaving the car windows partially down, she walked up the path to the restored barn that was now being put to such good use. She opened the heavy wooden door and stepped inside. Monsieur Albert was sitting at a cluttered desk.

When he saw who had entered, he jumped up and greeted her warmly.

"Madame Dufours! *Quelle surprise!* What can I do for you today? And how are *les chiots*? I will always see them as pups!"

"They are hardly pups now," Kat replied, with a chuckle. "You must come to the car to see them before I leave. How are you and your dear wife?"

"*Merci de demander*," he said, quickly making the sign of the cross and looking skyward through the open door. "Thank you for asking. We are well, *grâce à Dieu!*"

"I am so pleased to hear that. Is Delphine here?"

His smile faded and he wrung his hands. "*Hélas*, no ..." He paused and shifted uncomfortably in his seat, saying nothing more.

"We haven't heard from her for a week and are concerned," Kat said. "Is she unwell? Where is she?"

He gestured to a straight-backed chair by his desk. "Please, call me Raymond. *Asseyez-vous*, sit, and I will tell you what I know. I also am worried, but did not want to break Delphine's confidences in me. She made me swear to secrecy, but I think now the time for that is over." He crossed himself once again and gazed at the ceiling for several seconds before asking Kat whether she would like a coffee.

"*Non, merci.* Please just tell me what this is all about."

Raymond's face flushed and he cleared his throat loudly, his discomfort apparent. "I will start at the beginning. Delphine appeared at the door of the shelter one morning two years ago. She hoped to find work and offered to volunteer in exchange for room and board. She was calm on the surface, but we sensed there was a problem."

"Did it take long for her to open up to you?" Katherine hoped he would go into detail.

"After a week or two with the animals here, she began to relax. You know they touch her in a special way, as she does them. She began to trust us then too. Delphine has secrets and they are vital for her safety. Now I feel I must share them with you. I know you care about her."

A sharp pang of worry went straight to Katherine's core. This was not what she had expected.

"First of all, her real name is not Delphine. But that is how she wants to be known for the rest of her life. Right now, her given name is not important, but in time I will disclose it if need be. She comes from a remote village in the Pas de Calais, a department north of Paris, and from an early age she was a ward of the state. Her mother was unwed and, tragically, died when Delphine was just eight years old. Thank goodness she seems to have been a devoted mother who gave her daughter a foundation of love. But Delphine has no other family. *Pauvre jeune fille*." His eyes grew watery and he pulled out a large handkerchief to blow his nose.

Kat nodded, her sympathy obvious in the quiet tone of her voice. "Delphine did allude to this at Christmas when she was with us. She impressed upon us how much she appreciated being welcomed into our family. Go on, please."

"Life is not always fair, *non*? Some children are fortunate to be taken into the heart of a loving family and grow up with security, feeling valued and respected. Others ..." His voice died away and he again blew his nose and dabbed at his eyes.

"What happened to Delphine?"

"She had a series of horrible experiences with people who were not kind to her, including some things I cannot bring myself to repeat. I believe it was only because my dear wife, Marceline, was with us that first morning that she began to confide in us. As she held her hand, Delphine confessed she was fearful and in the process of running away. We wanted to help her and we were able to offer her a safe place to live as well as work." Raymond paused again.

Kat held her breath, willing him to continue.

"Her story came out gradually, over months, as she built her trust in us. The last foster family gave—but, really, sold, she found out later—Delphine, then only fifteen years old, to an 'uncle.' He told her she was going to help look after his aging parents but would also still be able to go to school. Then he drove her somewhere in a van for a day and a night."

Katherine felt as though ice water was being poured into her veins. She felt nauseated and angry at the same time. Hearing that this had happened to someone she cared for made it impossible for her to process the news calmly.

"She said he was kind to her and made her feel safe. He let her pick the music on the radio, bought her a nice dinner and talked to her about what she wanted to do when she grew up. She thought perhaps this would be a good situation for a change. Eventually they arrived at a large house at the edge of a town, near train tracks. As soon as she was inside, she found out that he had been lying to her. In reality, she had become the newest addition to a group of teenaged girls in the grip of a human trafficking ring. The girls were forced to perform in a local strip club and provide 'services' that had nothing to do with dancing. The 'club' was in a building attached to the back of the house. They were prisoners."

Katherine's eyes welled with tears, and she reached for a tissue. The story Raymond was telling was breaking her heart. *Poor, dear Delphine ...*

She could see Raymond was carefully choosing his words to deliver a clear picture of this young girl's history while leaving out the horrifying details that needed no description.

His voice dropped to an even softer tone, as he continued, "But in spite of all this, Delphine sometimes thought there would be an end to the horror. That maybe her pimp was not lying when he told her he was saving her money for her future. Imagine feeling so desperate that you could believe this. When she saw girls heartlessly beaten or pumped full of drugs for trying to leave ... or even for talking about it ... she knew there was no end in sight."

Katherine held up her hands and blew out a long breath. "Say no more. How on earth did she get away from this?"

"It was only through her wits, and the stupidity on the part of her captors, that she was able to escape after over a year of unspeakable abuse." His eyes filled with tears again. He lowered his head and stopped talking for a moment.

Kat shuddered, then touched his arm to express her empathy.

"*Excusez-moi*," Raymond apologized. He took a deep breath to regain his composure and continued. "One evening, she feigned illness. But instead of going to her room, she hid in a back closet of the club where she had concealed some clothes. After the doors closed for the night, she managed to steal a substantial amount of cash which she knew was kept in a bag under the bar. It was enough to buy a train ticket to Marseille and food. She left without anything other than a few items of clothing, which she wore layered until she was far enough away that she felt safe buying a bag for them. She had no identification. She did the obvious at first by cutting and coloring her hair in the bathroom of the train.

"She said she pretended to sleep most of the way to

Lyon, where she had to change trains, and that her heart was practically beating out of her chest from the fear of being retaken. Can you imagine?"

Kat absorbed all the details quietly as Raymond explained how Delphine had left the train in Marseille and found a sympathetic ear at a youth hostel. Someone at the desk had heard the stories of other teenagers arriving without identification and helped her get to the proper ministry office. There she filled in the copious paperwork needed to redeem her birth certificate.

Once she had something to identify her, she left Marseille. She had heard stories of sex trafficking in large port cities and did not want to stay there. She took the coastal train and got off in Cannes, planning to disappear into the countryside until she could decide what to do. She figured she was as far away from danger as she could be.

Raymond stopped talking now and stared intently at Katherine, who was speechless.

"What a terrible way to begin a life," she said at last. "The scars Delphine must be carrying with her! And yet somehow her sweet nature has survived."

"She is strong and fiercely independent, but with pain in her heart that endures." Raymond said. "She told us she had decided during the wait for her birth certificate that she would not let fear rule her life."

Neither of them said anything for a moment. It was almost too much for Kat to absorb. It didn't seem real. She had heard about the sex trade but had never imagined it would ever affect her in any way. Yet now it had affected her profoundly. To think of what Delphine must have gone through was unbearable.

In a quiet voice, Raymond continued. "She said her idea, once she got to Cannes, was to take a local bus and get off where she saw beauty. She wanted that beauty to define her from then on. And you know—we all know—this is how we met our sweet Delphine."

There was no question, Katherine thought, that in the few months she'd known Delphine, she had always seemed serene and at peace despite the completely different impression her appearance gave.

"Raymond, I was so surprised the first time I came here and saw Delphine dressed head to toe in that dark Goth clothing. She had more tattoos and piercings than anyone I had ever seen before. I felt quite intimidated until she spoke."

Raymond smiled wryly in agreement. "She told us how she changed her appearance on the train, dyeing her hair black and cutting it ragged. Then she went to the market in Marseille for her clothes, tattoos and piercings, which made her completely unrecognizable. But it was not just a disguise. It was also a statement of defiance and revenge over her past."

"And you helped her start her new life."

"She asked to volunteer in return for a place to sleep. We had the room at the back of the refuge. It was clear from the beginning that she loved working with the animals. She was a gift to us here, and still is. We were happy to have her stay as an employee."

Katherine was filled with questions. "Was she not traumatized by all she had been through? Is she still living here at the shelter?"

Raymond patiently provided the answers. "Traumatized? How does one determine what is under the surface? *Formidable!* But from the day she arrived, she was strong and determined to build a life here. That is the core of the Delphine we have come to know. At first we put a cot in the

storage room in the shelter. You know how rambling a struc-
ture it is and those thick stone walls help keep the tempera-
ture right."

"And she was content to stay there?"

"Not simply content. Every day Delphine would tell us
how safe and happy she felt. When she agreed to stay and
work for us, we tried to create a cozy space for her that she
could call home. Slowly she did. Come and see."

They walked through the large open space that held
the crates for the animals. A chorus of dogs barking and
cats yowling greeted them, and Kat smiled as Raymond
calmed them with hand gestures, pats and soft words.
"They like me, but Delphine is the Pied Piper here, *une
vraie Mère Teresa*. She works magic with animals, as you
know."

Kat smiled, knowing how gentle Delphine had been
with Rocco and Coco, nursing them as pups and helping to
save them from almost certain death. When she and
Philippe had adopted them, it had been the beginning of
their friendship with Delphine. In the months since then,
their friendship had grown into something special. She had
truly become a part of their family—this new family of Kat's
that was growing organically in France.

Raymond opened the door to Delphine's room at the
back of the shelter. Sunlight flooded into the space from two
deeply set windows, framed by the heavy stone walls. The
unfinished wood rafters and terra cotta floor tiles added to
the rustic ambiance. Two other walls were whitewashed
plaster and covered in brightly painted whimsical flowers
and animals. What surprised Kat was the easel set up by
one window and the paint tubes and brushes on a box next
to it. Then she realized that Delphine must have painted the
pictures on the walls and also the many canvases, some

propped two deep at the bases of the walls, also depicting animals and landscapes.

"When we knew that Delphine was going to stay and work here, we had the cement floor tiled and installed the heat and air-conditioning unit above the door. She has added her special touches to make it her home. *C'est mignon, non? Très agréable!*"

Katherine could feel the love that filled this room and nodded in agreement. Delphine had put her heart into every detail.

"I didn't realize she was an artist too!" she exclaimed. "It makes me so happy to see how settled she is here. I often wondered how she was managing on her own. Now what can we do to find her? Do you have any idea where she is?"

Raymond frowned. "*Désolé, non, pas cette fois*. This time is different. She would occasionally go away on her days off, but never for more than two days."

"Do you know where she would go? And why?"

"I only know that there's a safe house somewhere between here and Nice for young women. In the hills. The location is highly confidential. When a girl arrives there, the supervisor texts Delphine. She tries to help by talking to the girls and also by answering the emergency hotline. But for her to be gone for five days and not contact us makes us very worried."

"Does Delphine carry any identification with her?"

"She eventually gave us her true identity papers for safe-keeping and over time she acquired cards—for the train, for the gym—with her new name. Enough to use in her daily life. Her greatest fear was that someone would track her down. We gave her a business card with her new name and our phone number."

Without realizing it, Kat and Raymond had both been

pacing nervously as they spoke. Now Raymond suggested they go back to his office. Once there, Kat still did not sit down.

"This is frustrating," she said. "I think we should contact the police. Maybe they know where the safe house is."

Raymond shrugged. "Perhaps, as her employer, it makes sense for me to do this. *Mais honnêtement*, I do not think we should reveal her true name. I have to honor my promise to her. At least for now."

Katherine was silent as she considered the gravity of the situation. Then she said, "Let me call Philippe and see what he suggests. For reasons that are too crazy for me to even begin to explain right now, we have some connection with high ranking police in Nice and Paris. Who knows. They may be able to help."

Raymond looked relieved by her offer. "Perhaps you are right. We were talking only this morning about whether we should call the police."

She took out her phone and tapped Philippe's number. He answered immediately. "*Mon coeur*, I've been worried. Is Delphine sick? What have you found out?"

Kat gave him a short version of everything Raymond had told her. Philippe interjected from time to time with moans of concern and murmurs of disbelief. When she asked his advice about calling the police, he agreed that it was the right thing to do and said he would call their contact in Nice, Inspecteur Thibidault, to find out the best way to begin searching for Delphine. "We can't do any better than to begin at the top. Why don't you come home now, and I will get things started."

atherine left Raymond with the assurance that she would let him know the minute she and Philippe had anything to report. "We must all try not to worry too much. We must believe this will be resolved in the best possible way."

She gestured toward the car, "Come and see how our beauties have grown since they left you."

The dogs were happy to be let out of the car and dashed around the yard after greeting Raymond. Kat hoped they would be on their best behavior, and they did not let her down. After racing each other to fetch the ball Raymond kept throwing down the yard, they looked ready to drop and settled down in the back of the car for the drive home. Kat repeated her promise to call Raymond as soon as she learned anything and said goodbye.

She caught herself shaking her head in shock most of the way home. A knot had formed in her stomach, and she felt queasy. Delphine's story was difficult for her to process. She could not imagine how anyone could go through years of neglect and abuse and still become a compassionate young woman. She had to stop on the narrow shoulder of the road twice to wipe away the tears that threatened to blind her.

Philippe phoned when Kat was half way home and she pulled off the road again to answer the call. Philippe told her that he had left a message for Thibidault and hoped to hear back soon. He also said that he had left a similar message with an old friend who worked undercover in the area around Nice. He might have some inside information that could help.

"*Tu vas bien?*" Philippe asked. "It must have been difficult to listen to the details of this terrible story. *Pauvre* Delphine!"

"I feel so unsettled. I keep crying when I think about all that Delphine has endured. I can't imagine the strength it must have taken her to rise above it. I just want her to be safe. I can't bear to accept anything else."

"*Fais attention*. Drive carefully. I'm waiting for you."

"I'm going to stop at Simone's first. She needs to hear this in person. I know how difficult this will be for her."

Before she got back on the road, Katherine called to let Simone know she would be there shortly.

"I know there's a problem, or I would have heard from you right away," Simone said, her voice thick with worry. "So I've been painting to keep my mind off whatever it is. I will get cleaned up and meet you in the kitchen. The door is not locked."

A scent of orange and cinnamon, perhaps also rose hips, greeted Kat as she opened the front door. After sharing so many pots of tea with Simone, she was beginning to recognize her magic potions. The smell was instantly calming, and Kat inhaled it deeply before going into the kitchen.

Simone was sitting at the table, lifting a cozy from one of

her many teapots. Tilting her face to accept Katherine's *bises*, she greeted her warmly before filling their cups.

Kat sighed loudly and rubbed her hands over her face before she started to relate what Raymond had told her.

Simone listened quietly, her lips pursed. At times she closed her eyes and nodded slowly.

"After Delphine opened up to us, somewhat, at *la fête de Noël*, I'm saddened but not surprised to learn this about her past life," Simone said once Kat had finished her tale. "However, hearing that she was used by human traffickers is the worst possible news. That sweet girl robbed of her innocence. And trust her to want to help others as a result of her experience. Now we must find her."

Kat nodded. "Philippe has already put in a call to Inspecteur Thibidault. Hopefully he can steer us in the right direction. He must know who to contact at headquarters. Honestly, Simone, we are so fortunate to have that connection with him through you and Nick. The police should be on the case by tonight."

"Yes, he is a person of influence at the highest level of criminal investigation, *bien sûr!*"

"It was a bizarre coincidence that Nick first put us in touch with him. And then it turned out you and Thibidault had this close connection, which we still don't know all about, I might add." Kat gave Simone a quizzical look.

Simone's expression gave nothing away. "Patience, *chérie*. One day everything will be revealed." Then she became solemn once more. "From what you say, Delphine texted Monsieur Albert on Tuesday to say that she was returning and then never did. Today is Thursday. We have two days that need to be explained. I don't like this."

∼

That evening, around eleven, Kat took her cell phone to the bedroom. She made herself comfortable on the window seat and tapped Molly's number in Toronto. It was dinner time there and she hoped Molly would be home and up for a video chat.

"Yay! What a pleasant surprise." Her best friend's throaty voice always made Kat smile. What made her laugh out loud was the sight of Molly's big eyes peering at her from a face obviously undergoing some sort of treatment. It was completely covered in something unidentifiable.

"I'm so glad I caught you ..., but where have I caught you?" Kat asked. "What's with the face mask? Are you at a spa?"

"Yes! My very own home spa. This is a turmeric, mashed banana and honey mask that will give me radiant skin and make me look years younger! Well, maybe not, but it smells good enough to eat. I should just add peanut butter to it!"

Kat laughed, but quickly became serious.

Molly sensed the change in mood. "What's up, girl-friend? This isn't our usual call day."

"Oh Molly!" Kat sniffed loudly and her face crumpled. "We all are so upset. Delphine is missing!"

"What do you mean? Like, poof, she has vanished?"

"Seriously, that's about it," Kat said, trying to pull herself together. "She and Simone have talked on the phone a couple of times a week since Christmas. But this morning, Simone told me that Delphine didn't call last week. She was concerned, as every time she tried to reach her she only got her voicemail. So I went to Mougins this afternoon to see if she was sick."

Kat went on to relate a short version of what Monsieur Albert had told her.

Molly's eyes widened and her jaw dropped bit by bit as

she listened. When Kat had finished, she asked, "Are the police on it? This is terrible! From what you say of her past life, someone may have tracked her down. That definitely sounded like human trafficking with that sick fu ... erm ... douchebag—oops, I was about to say worse—who called himself her uncle. What a pig! Those evil people will stop at nothing!"

Kat found that telling the story had made her tense up even more. "I agree. We're afraid that somehow someone from her past managed to find her even with her new identity. Philippe keeps telling me I should focus on the positive until bad news changes everything. So that's what I'm trying to do. It's so hard. But I just keep reminding myself how smart and strong Delphine is."

Even under the mask, Molly looked thoughtful. "It's bizarre you mention this now. Human trafficking in Toronto is becoming "epidemic." That's a direct quote from the newspaper today. We have police coming on a regular basis to the church shelter we run to talk to us."

"I'm shocked," Kat exclaimed. "I wonder if it is like that here on the Riviera too. I never really thought much about it. I mean, I would read the odd article online or in the paper but did not pay a lot of attention to it. Now I feel like an idiot."

Molly said, "But the Delphine I met doesn't fit the stereotype of most victims we read about. Insecure, vulnerable, without a voice—young women who don't have a platform or the courage or the means to say no and run away. Tony and I hear about it time and again at our youth shelter, when someone is able to break free. Or worse yet, some are tossed back out on the street like trash, often addicted to drugs. I wonder—"

"But she once was like that, now that we know her past,"

Kat interrupted. "I'm sure that is why she has been trying to help others—been there, done that—but she was lucky enough to keep her wits about her and escape and make a new start."

Molly nodded and completed her previous thought. "So the question is whether she has been trapped again or if she is helping somebody somewhere."

"It's a waiting game, and it's horrible. I keep imagining her being forced back into some hellish situation or," Kat gulped, "being trafficked away from here to some other country even." She wiped tears away with her hand.

Molly offered comforting words, asked about Simone, and promised to call in the next day or two. "I'll let you know as soon as we hear anything at all," Katherine assured her.

"Pffft!" Molly exclaimed. "Call me whenever ... news or no news. I wish I could be right there with you, but this is the next best thing."

"You're right, Moll. It helps so much to talk to you. Give Tony a hug from me. Love you guys."

"Rightbackatcha and to Philippe. Love you both. I know you will not be able to stop worrying. It's only natural."

Katherine reached over to turn off the lamp on the side table. She stayed on the window seat, looking out over the garden, the moonlight washing over her. After a few minutes, she placed a video call to her cousin Andrea on her organic farm an hour away from Toronto. Besides Molly, Andrea was her closest friend and always a voice of calm and reason. They called each other regularly. She had met Delphine when she and her husband Terrance were at Kat and Philippe's wedding. Kat thought that she should know about this too.

Andrea was as shocked as Molly had been as Kat related

what had happened. They spoke for a half hour. Andrea listened thoughtfully and tried to help Kat feel hopeful. She had read the same news report as Molly and expressed her concerns about the rise of this trafficking problem in their own back yard.

"Our yoga club has a strong meditation group that focuses on prayers and blessings, sending pure energy where it is most needed. I'll ask that we focus our intentions and send pure energy to where she is. It's powerful, Kat. We won't give up."

They promised to talk again in a few days. When the call was over, Kat was glad she had talked with both friends. But now she felt empty. Drained and hurting.

Before she went to bed, she peeked in on Belle and her brood, who were all sound asleep in one big furry ball. Even that peaceful scene brought her no relief.

Philippe was in bed reading. "I'm glad you had a chance to chat with Molly and Andrea. Keep reaching out to them for support. Come to bed, *Minou*, and let me wipe those tears."

As she slipped under the light duvet and nestled into Philippe's arms, Kat lost control and wept. "I'm so afraid!"

"*Pleure pas, mon coeur*," Philippe whispered. "Don't cry." He kissed the tears from her face and held her close. "We will be strong together. Try to sleep now. *Je t'adore*."

5

That night was a sleepless one for Kat. She was so worried about what might have happened to Delphine she just tossed and turned, trying not to wake Philippe.

On Friday, Inspector Thibidault returned Philippe's call and gave him the name and contact number of the person in charge of the Human Trafficking Enforcement Unit. "Inspector Guy Marchand is waiting for your call."

Inspector Marchand told Philippe that Monsieur Albert needed to register a missing person's report before the police in Nice could open a file on the case and put officers to work on finding her. After that, Philippe and the Alberts exchanged several texts and phone calls to ensure this was completed. Raymond went to his local *gendarmerie* to fill out forms and an official investigation was begun.

On Saturday morning there still was no news of Delphine's whereabouts. After another sleepless night, Kat's eyes filled with tears as she talked with Philippe about her fears. "It all seems so frightening and hopeless."

"*Je comprends, Minou,*" Philippe murmured. "I understand exactly how it makes you feel. I'm fighting those thoughts as well. But the police say the next logical step is to widen the circle of people looking for Delphine. An alert is being sent out from the headquarters in Paris. It must be done, and hopefully it will bring her back to us."

"I feel so helpless—useless—like I should be doing something. But what? I keep envisioning tattered black and white posters with Delphine's photo and information, like the countless posters I've seen through the years of missing girls and women. It makes me want to cry for her—for them."

"*Je t'assure*—trust me—we are doing all we can. The police are involved at the highest level. We have to keep hoping and praying and believing all will turn out well. Come, walk with me to the bottom of the garden, then we must get ready to go to Carnaval."

Philippe took Kat's hand. He lifted it to his lips and kissed it as they crossed the lawn. They stopped now and then to see what green shoots were emerging in the expansive flower beds.

"Auguste was here this morning, turning the soil and working his magic," Kat said. "He's coming back later today with a load of hydrangea bushes to plant and will let the dogs out then for a quick run."

They stood at the stone wall, looking out across the water, now calm after a week of crashing waves. The air felt crisp, but the sun was warm and a welcome change from the recent rainy days. Rocco and Coco bounded around them, dropping sticks to be thrown and making Kat smile in spite of her sadness.

"Doesn't the sun feel good on our faces?" Philippe said. "Let's soak it in, take that positivity and have as happy a day as we possibly can."

They walked back to the house hand in hand, and the dogs settled down on their beds in the mudroom. Kat made certain the door to the closet in the master bedroom was open, as Belle had decided that was home for her brood for now.

Soon they were driving along the Bord de Mer, following the coast to Nice under a stunning azure sky. The sea was calm and sparkled under the late morning sun.

"It's such a beautiful day, *Minou*." Philippe said. "Let's try to relax and enjoy ourselves. We've been dedicated to finding Delphine for two days and we need to take a little break from worry. We need to focus on hope."

"I'll try not to be consumed with worry about Delphine today. I know the police are doing their best to find her and I have to be patient. I can't tell you how many times I've said that to myself since I got up this morning."

"*C'est plus facile à dire qu'à faire,*" Philippe replied.

"Yes. Easier said than done. It's hard not to think about her. It's the unknown that is so difficult ..."

As they stopped for a red light, their eyes met in shared understanding. "They will find her," they said in unison.

She squeezed his hand. "We have to keep believing."

They drove along in silence for a while, each occupied by their own thoughts.

Kat tried to calm herself by changing the subject when she next spoke. "I'm so glad Marcel could help Gilles at the market this morning. It's not often I get to have your company for an entire Saturday. I am so looking forward to Carnaval!"

Philippe smiled. "David texted that he and Véronique will meet us by their favorite stall for *les bugnes* or what I call *ganses*. We decided that this has to be your first carnival treat."

"And they are?"

"Delicious! *Gansa* is the name in the Niçois language, but most people refer to them as *beignets de Carnaval*. They're a deep-fried light pastry, sprinkled with powdered sugar, kind of like some of those doughnuts you had me sample in Toronto last year, your 'Timbits,' but better."

Kat poked him lightly in the ribs and smiled at the memory.

He continued. "Just like at the *marché de Noël*, there are all sorts of food stalls. We thought we would simply graze them for lunch. We can sample the wares and browse the vendors until the Parade of Flowers starts around two-thirty. We scored good seats in the viewing stands in Place Masséna, where it all begins."

Traffic slowed to a crawl as they drew closer to Nice. Philippe turned off the Boulevard des Anglais and navigated the narrow back streets he knew so well. They were soon parked in the old town and walking to their meeting spot. Philippe was shouldering a light backpack with a blanket, hats and gloves inside.

"We may need them this evening when we watch the Parade of Lights," Kat had insisted. "Once the sun sets, it's going to be cool."

Philippe sighed with exasperation as they stood in line to pass through the security cordon, and Katherine squeezed his hand. Ever since the tragic attack in Nice on Bastille Day just a few years earlier, the security check had been required. "Nothing is as easy to access as it used to be," Philippe grumbled, "but for good reason. They will need to inspect this bag. So we have to get in the right line. It's simply a shame."

"An unfortunate sign of the times," Kat agreed.

Soon enough they were through the gates and walking

past the extravagantly decorated stalls that lined the Promenade du Paillon in the Jardin Albert 1er. Vendors, some in elaborate or outrageous costumes, were selling crazy hats, masks and bags of confetti, as well as snacks and soft drinks.

Wide-eyed, Katherine kept swiveling her head at the sight of so many musicians, clowns, stilt walkers and face painters. She was surprised by how many people were in costume. "And so many children have dressed up. It's like Hallowe'en at home."

"Everyone who wears a costume gets in free," Philippe told her, pointing at one of the more hilarious outfits.

"And what are those massive papier-mâché heads? They're insanely big!"

"That's exactly what those costumes are called," Philippe said. "*Les Grosses Têtes*. Big heads."

Some of the big heads were caricatures of politicians and celebrities they recognized, which made them laugh. Kat already had her camera at the ready, and Philippe waited patiently while she captured image after irresistible image.

The atmosphere was loud and joyful, and the air was sweet with smells wafting from food stalls and great barrels of *vin chaud*. As they neared the first stand, they heard David's cheery voice hailing them above the growing roar of the crowd. They pushed their way through a large group of spectators and met with their friends. Véronique held out a paper bag with the tasty pastries inside. "Here. *Les bugnes* for you. *Bienvenue à Carnaval!*"

"These are scrumptious!" Kat exclaimed after her first bite, which left her with a sugary mustache. Philippe gently brushed it away.

After an hour of sauntering past displays and munching

on socca, Nice's traditional chickpea crepe, the four friends made their way to their seats in the grandstand.

As the men chatted, Véronique explained to Katherine how they could have walked alongside the parade in the crowd of pedestrians. "It's totally chaotic and actually great fun but we can do that another year. We thought for your first time at Carnaval we should sit in the stands. It will take longer to watch everything pass by but you won't miss a thing."

"That sounds good. I read somewhere that the parade is also called the Battle of the Flowers. Any reason?"

"That was the original name, *Bataille des Fleurs*," Philippe said. "And the first one was in 1876."

Véronique laughed. "From everything I've read, things used to get pretty crazy back in the day. But that was then and this is now—much calmer."

"*D'accord*," David said. "Now the battle part is just that tons of flowers are thrown from elaborate floats by women dressed in exquisite costumes. Kat, you'll collect a beautiful bouquet as the parade passes by."

Véronique added, her eyes bright with excitement, "*Honnêtement*, you will be amazed at the quantity of flowers of all kinds. *C'est spectaculaire!*"

"Four thousand flowers on each float, I read," David said. "Which, of course, is a great boon to the local economy each year as 80% are grown in greenhouses throughout the region."

For two hours, the action was non-stop, loud and laughter-filled. A steady parade of fantastic blossom-covered floats topped with giant balloons rolled across Place Masséna and down through the park to the Promenade. All the flowers grown along the Riviera were represented, especially mimosas, gerberas, daisies, gladioli, roses, and carnations. Clowns, dancers, stilt walkers and other riders dressed in colorful, flamboyant costumes tossed stems and branches to the crowd from the floats. Some people wore voluminous gowns made from dozens of meters of fabric, while others wore bejeweled bikinis and towering, feathered head gear. Between the floats came brightly dressed marching bands. The costumes, the constant shower of flowers, streamers and confetti, and the towering balloons against the bright blue sky did what they were meant to do—they chased the winter blues away.

By the end of the riotous event, all four friends were hoarse from laughing and trying to make themselves heard above the noise. Kat and Véronique had each gathered a huge, fragrant bouquet.

The two couples strolled back to David and Véronique's home in the heart of the old town. Kat loved their apartment in one of the oldest medieval buildings in Nice.

"I've been meaning to ask you about Delphine," Véronique said as they neared the building, "but I'm going to wait until we are all settled inside."

Katherine smiled weakly. "Yes, let's wait."

Once they were inside the front door, David gestured for them to sit in the salon *"C'est l'heure de l'apéro!"* he declared, and they all decided a glass of pastis was called for.

"There's something soothing about this drink," Kat said, as Philippe added water to her glass. "I love the way the clear amber becomes milky as the water is added. It's almost magical. Did you know, I had never even heard of pastis or pernod until I came to France? And what's stranger is that I cannot stand eating black licorice but I love that same flavor in this drink. How weird is that?"

David said, "Well, it is called *the* apéritif of Provence for good reason. There are few people who are not reminded of the south of France when they take a sip. And, by the way, Kat, I had never heard of this drink either until Véronique kidnapped me and brought me to France!"

Véronique rolled her eyes and passed around an olive-wood tray arrayed with tapenade on small toasts and bite-sized rounds of saucisson d'Arles. After they had each taken one of the hors d'oeuvres, she set the tray on the coffee table beside a bowl filled with roasted almonds.

David entertained them with a few amusing anecdotes about how his classic American life in Boston changed when he married Véronique, who was from France but had been studying in New York for a few years. After they married they moved to Lyons and then Nice. There were many funny stories, but David never seemed to repeat any of them.

The fun of the carnival and being with good friends had the intended effect on Kat, who now felt quite relaxed.

"*Santé!* And belated words of love for *la Saint Valentin* two days ago!" David toasted.

"Honestly," Kat said, "we've been so preoccupied and worried about Delphine that we barely noticed Valentine's Day."

Philippe kissed Kat's cheek. "Every day is *la Saint Valentin* for us, *mon coeur.*"

David gave Véronique a sideways look. "I was just about to say that to you, darling! Philippe managed to own those words before I got to them, Casanova that he is!"

They raised their glasses in a toast. But Katherine was suddenly seized again with worry about Delphine.

Véronique sensed a problem. "Is Delphine sick, Kat? We haven't spoken since you texted me you were going to Mougins to check on her."

Katherine was apologetic. "Oh Véronique—and David—

this whole situation has been so stressful. I meant to call you, but we decided to wait until we were together to talk about it. We hoped that, in the meantime, everything would be resolved in a good way. But it's not."

She and Philippe took turns recounting what Raymond Albert had told her. Véronique quickly moved to Kat's side and slipped her arm around her. "Oh, I am so sorry. I can imagine how concerned you have been. You should have called me."

"Naturally," Kat said, her voice breaking with emotion, "we started thinking of all the bad things that might have happened. Did someone from her past life recognize her? Has she been taken somewhere? Is she hurt? I called Philippe right away from Mougins ..."

Philippe took her hand and picked up the story. "Then I spoke with Thibidault, whom you know, and he got right through to the department involved with missing women. They sent someone up to the shelter in Mougins to talk to Monsieur and Madame Albert after Raymond filled out a missing person report."

"No time wasted there!" David exclaimed.

"Raymond Albert called me after the police left. He said it was very upsetting at first for them," Kat said. "The police officer almost made them feel responsible for Delphine's disappearance. Then they suggested that it was her choice to leave and not say anything. That possibly she did not want to be connected with them anymore." Her voice rose as her words spilled out, venting her frustration and anger. "How could they suggest such a thing?"

Philippe patted her hand. "*Calme-toi, chérie.* You know they were simply doing their job, and those are legitimate questions for the police to ask. They did not know the personal connections with Delphine at first. And, even so, it's just our word as far as they are concerned."

"Monsieur and Madame Albert were beside themselves at the idea that Delphine had decided to leave without telling them," Katherine said.

"The police were far more positive about the possibility she didn't leave voluntarily after learning about Delphine's history," Philippe added.

"Yes, once they learned how close we all were, they treated us with more respect. When we told them that she had been helping at an undisclosed—to us anyway—safe house for runaways, they took a different approach. They said it could be that she is stuck at the safe house trying to help. Apparently at some of those places, because security is of the utmost importance, you have to hand in your cell phone when you arrive. It is then locked away. That's so girls or women who are there can't try to contact their pimps or other controllers if they have second thoughts, which often happens."

"So you mean Delphine could be in a kind of lockdown with no means of communication?" Véronique asked.

"That was the suggestion," Kat replied. "It kind of makes us feel better, in a weird way. With all your contacts in Nice, have either of you ever heard any mention of a safe house for runaway girls in the area? Or talk of human trafficking happening along the coast?"

David was quick to respond. "With the current migrant crisis in most countries bordering the Mediterranean, there are countless related issues. It's a shocking ongoing situation. There has always been trafficking with young women from eastern Europe and north Africa, and programs fighting the sex trade, including domestic."

Véronique's green eyes flashed with anger. "About ten

years ago there was a dreadful case in the north of a large ring of French men who had enslaved women as prostitutes. It was a terrible situation, and there were many arrests and convictions. It seems to be a scourge on society that doesn't go away. It's so disturbing!"

David mentioned the Association Assistance et Recherche de Personnes Disparues. "Also known as the ARPD, it's an association that helps search for people who have disappeared. Perhaps they should be contacted."

Kat and Philippe looked at each other. "Everything is worth trying," he said.

"Let's look up their contact information right now," David said, reaching for his tablet.

When they found the website, Katherine sent the association an email requesting contact, and Philippe phoned to leave a voicemail in French.

"There! Let's hope something comes of it," Véronique said. "Now, let's try to focus on the positive and in the joys of David's cooking."

Having finished their apéros, they moved to the dining table, already set with gleaming china and crystal wine glasses.

"David creates more comfort and joy in the kitchen than anyone I have ever met," Kat said. "And the fact that he makes this magic in a space the size of a closet never ceases to amaze me!"

David smiled. "You know it's my passion!"

"*Grâce à Dieu!*" Véronique interjected. "Because we all know I don't cook."

"*Grâce à Dieu!*" David echoed, and they all laughed. Véronique's failed attempts at preparing family dinners were legendary, and David and their children often told stories about them. Her successful career as a weaver took up all of her passion and time, and her family was proud of her.

David called from behind the screen that partially hid the tiny kitchen, "Since I knew there would be *beaucoup de snacking* today, I've kept the meal simple. It's something I know we all love. A sure way to collect compliments!"

He carried in a steaming cast iron pot of mussels in a rich tomato, thyme and garlic broth. The aroma filled the room, drawing gasps of pleasure from Katherine and Philippe.

Véronique followed with a bowl of frites that had been dusted with parmesan and parsley. A fresh baguette rested on an olive-wood board.

"What more could we ask for?" Philippe said, and Kat applauded.

*a*fter they had eaten and cleared the dishes away, they lingered at the table.

"Let's not get too comfortable," Véronique said. "We should be heading back for *le Corso Carnavalesque Illumine.* Are you ready? Is everyone well-fortified?"

"That's the Parade of Lights," Philippe translated for Kat, giving her a wink. "We need to make sure you know the correct names of all these things as you transform into *une vraie française.*"

"I'm a constant work in progress, *mon chou,*" Katherine said, grinning back.

"Having been through the process myself a lifetime ago, I would say you are progressing very well indeed," David said, putting his arm over her shoulder and giving her a gentle hug.

They had all been friends for over a year now, ever since Kat and Philippe's fateful first trip to Entrevaux. David had frequently regaled them with tales of his adjustment to French life after he and Véronique moved from the States.

"You're my role model, David," Kat said. "I've learned a

lot from all the stories you and Véronique have told me about your early years as an Anglophone in France."

David chuckled. "Trust me. There are more."

He finished filling two thermoses with *vin chaud*. "Some additional sustenance so no one has to leave our seats in the stands for a hot drink. It could get chilly."

Kat said thanks to whoever had arranged the gallery seats. "As much as it looked like the people milling about on the sidelines this afternoon were having fun, I'm glad we will be snugly settled wrapped in our blankets in the bleachers tonight."

Then the four friends put on their coats, hats and gloves and set out.

There was a steady flow of people through the narrow alleys of the old town as a growing crowd made its way up to Place Masséna. By the time the four of them were seated, blaring music was announcing the beginning of the procession—the arrival of the king.

As they waited for that first float to appear, Philippe and David took turns telling Kat the story of how the Carnaval began.

"Records of a spring carnival in Nice go back to the 1200s," Philippe said. "But really, it began in the early 1800s—"

"1830 to be exact," David, the historian, corrected. "The king and queen of Sardinia were visiting Nice, and the city decided to put on a parade for them. They sat on the palace balcony and waved to the aristocrats passing by in their fancy carriages. Take it away, Philippe."

"Right. The next year someone made a king out of clothes stuffed with straw and put him on the balcony. Some years later, someone else decided the king should head up the parade, and it just grew from that."

Kat laughed, "I love these stories and traditions!"

Véronique said, "Now an enormous papier-mâché king leads the parade and watches over everything. Each year there is a beauty contest and a new queen is voted on. The different quarters of town get involved, and many neighborhoods hold their own parties and special events. In the early days, each part of the city would build a float in great secrecy and the competition among them was fierce. The theme of *le roi de carnaval* changes each year, and this year he is the King of Cinema. Several guest countries are invited to participate each year as well, which adds an exotic element. Should be fun!"

Philippe told Kat they should come back for the last night of the carnival. None of them would tell her what would happen then. "Let it be a surprise!"

After the Parade of Lights was over, Katherine had to admit she had never before seen anything like it. The afternoon parade had been impressive, but the imagination, creativity and gusto that passed before her during the evening's two-hour show went beyond her imagination.

The floats were massive, with towering balloon figures both animal and human. Some, along with the over one hundred *grosses têtes*, were hilarious caricatures of politicians and celebrities. A great deal of fun was poked at local, national and international events. As in the afternoon, each float was followed by dancers, acrobats, and musicians, many of them tossing sweets to the crowd.

There was *bombe serpentin* or crazy string everywhere. The floats were covered in it. Spectators shot the multicolored strands at them and were bombarded back from the floats. Kat was flabbergasted. Picking pieces of string from her hair, she shouted above the fray to Philippe, "This is crazy. I could do without this part!"

"You should see the floats by the end of the two weeks. They are completely covered!" he shouted back.

The interaction between the people on parade and their noisy spectators was constant, and the energy electric. Video of the passing floats was projected on enormous screens set up along the route—massive visuals of chaos, color and fun.

"This is sensory and visual overload," Kat cried at one point, her hands over her ears.

When the parade finally ended, the partying did not—and would not for some time, judging by the crowd's energy.

As they waited to join the throng climbing down from the stands, Katherine suddenly grabbed Philippe's arm and pointed to a young woman in the crowd on the street below who seemed to be accompanied by a scruffy middle-aged man. "Isn't that her? Delphine?"

She shouted as loudly as she could, "Delphine! Delphine!"

The woman did not respond at first. Then she took a quick glance in Katherine's direction, turned her head away just as quickly, and shuffled off into the crowd. Philippe sprang down the stand, jumping over the backs of seats, calling back to Kat to stay with Véronique and David, and ran in the direction the young woman had gone.

"I'm sure it was her," Kat said breathlessly to her friends. "Even though I only got a glimpse."

Twenty minutes later, Philippe returned alone, out of breath, and covered in crazy string.

"I followed them into the old town, but lost them in the crowd. It was impossible!"

"So was it really her?"

"Did you get a good look?"

"Did she see you?"

They peppered him with questions as he sat down and caught his breath. "I am certain it was Delphine, and, no, she did not see me following them. I phoned the direct line Thibidault sent me and reported who I was and what I was seeing. I was ordered to get away from the area as quickly as possible, because it is under surveillance and some planned action is about to take place."

Kat gasped. "What does that mean? Is Delphine going to be safe?"

"*Impossible à dire*," Philippe said, sounding testy and frustrated. "I cannot tell you anything from that incident. Maybe it was not her! There's always uncertainty when our imaginations are involved."

Dispirited by Philippe's news, the friends said goodnight, sharing their concern for Delphine's safety and wishing her well. Exhausted by the parade, Kat fell asleep in the car while Philippe drove them home.

7

*O*n Tuesday, Katherine had to force herself to follow through with the ski day she had signed up for weeks previously. It was with the expat women's group she had joined when she first settled in Antibes. This energetic international group had become an important part of Kat's transition to living in France and she enjoyed the company of all the women.

The problem was her ongoing worry about Delphine, who had now been gone for a week. She found it difficult to feel interested in doing anything.

Philippe encouraged her to go. "You will be glad once you get on your way. You always enjoy your time with these ladies."

"You're right," Kat said unenthusiastically. "I'm going to yoga first. Annette is going to meet me there."

"When you are on the bus, ask if anyone has any involvement with helping runaway girls," Philippe said. "Or if they know anyone remotely connected in some way to helping. There's a good possibility one or two will know something. And besides, it is going to be a beautiful day for skiing! You need a distraction."

"From one activity to another," Kat's friend Annette commented as they settled into their seats. They had both attended the 7:00 a.m. wake-up yoga class and then taken the train into Nice to catch this coach. With ski clothes in their backpacks, they would rent the rest of their equipment at the hill.

Isola 2000 was the nearest ski resort in the southern Alps, close to the Italian border and an hour and a half's drive due north of Nice.

As they set off, the driver announced that there had been a snowfall overnight and all runs were open and in good condition. The roads were clear, and the coach climbed easily up the heights of the Alpes-Maritimes.

Katherine had confided Delphine's situation to Annette while they were on the train. Now Annette reinforced Philippe's advice. "Kat, ask the driver if you can use his microphone to ask everyone if they have any information about runaway girls."

Katherine took a deep breath and went to ask the driver. She knew it was a good idea, no matter how difficult it would be to talk about it. The driver was happy to oblige, and Kat was amazed at the response from the women. A few of them said they volunteered with the ARPD, the organization that David had mentioned on the weekend.

The support and sympathy the women offered her buoyed Katherine's spirit. She felt the weight lift from her shoulders slightly, and the flame of hope for Delphine's safe return flickered more brightly.

The Alps' white peaks towered before them as the bus approached the ski area. Kat spotted a couple of eagles soaring high in the deep blue, cloudless sky and nudged Annette to take a look. They drove past timbered chalets tucked between alpine-styled inns and pedestrians wearing boots and jackets and carrying ski gear.

The coach driver reminded everyone to apply sunscreen. "At these high altitudes, you can very quickly get a bad sunburn."

Kat spent the rest of the journey studying the trail map with Annette, and by the time they arrived at the base lodge, they had their morning planned. Lunch was one of the most important details. Several of the women, including Kat and Annette, planned to meet at the restaurant in the rustic cabin partway up the mountain. Annette had told her earlier that the owners kept a donkey, and Kat had packed a bagful of carrots for it.

"We will bring greetings from Victor Hugo and the twins," Kat said now.

It had been a few years since Kat had been on skis, but it only took a few turns for her to feel comfortable again. The more exposed slopes were too icy for her to attempt, but the back slopes were in fine condition, with the fresh snow already groomed into a smooth carpet. The feeling of soaring down fresh snow exhilarated her. For a few hours Kat was able to lose herself in the beauty of the snow-covered Alps around her stretching majestically to the horizon.

She and Annette waited for each other at the bottom of the slopes and chatted about their runs while they rode the chair lifts and gondolas back to the top. From time to time, one or the other of them would let out a whoop of pleasure as they cruised a run in the warm sunshine. Before she knew it, the afternoon had flown by and it was time to get back on the bus.

"Today was amazing," Kat exclaimed as they settled once more into their seats on the coach. "Philippe kept saying we should come up here to one of the mountain ski resorts, but we hadn't made it yet. I'll have to come back with him."

On the way back to Nice, the coach stopped in a picturesque village, where the women capped off the day with dinner at a small bistro with a big reputation. Perched like an eagle's nest on a mountain ledge, the restaurant overlooked a deep valley that gave them a teasing glimpse of the Mediterranean, still an hour's drive away.

The meal was an experience in itself, with the young chef passionately reciting the provenance of the local ingredients and telling them about the 300-year-old communal bread oven in the village, in which he'd baked the bread that accompanied their meal.

"It's hard to believe this is just an hour and a half away from our lives on the Côte d'Azur, *n'est-ce pas*?" Kat said with a sigh, once they had settled back into their seats on the coach.

Annette nodded imperceptibly and promptly fell asleep. Most of the women on the bus were soon also dozing off, but Kat felt wide awake.

Suddenly, she felt a tap on her shoulder. A woman she knew slightly, Élise Fortier, leaned in and asked Kat to sit with her, a few rows back.

"I wanted to speak to you on the ride up after you told us about your friend. But I did not want to spoil the day for either of us, so I waited until now. I have a story to tell you. My daughter became caught up in a sex-trafficking disaster a few years ago. It was a nightmare and I hope I can share some important information with you."

Kat followed her to the back of the coach, and listened as Élise haltingly told her how her seventeen-year-old daughter, Chantal—an A-student and top athlete—had fallen prey to an online predator.

"He told her he was an agent for a well-known modeling company. She told us about him, and we checked his name and photo against the company's website. It seemed to be on the level. We advised her not to continue chatting with him, but she said he was nice and giving her good advice, encouraging her to stay in school."

This was a story Kat had heard before, or ones similar, but she had never met anyone who had lived through the experience and she was stunned at the intensity of Élise's pain. Not that it was unexpected, but that it was so raw, so deep. It resounded in every word and expression, every blink of her eyes. She was at a loss as to how to console her, but, without realizing it, the two women were already holding each other's hands.

"She kept in touch with him?" Kat asked.

"Yes, without us knowing. Then one Saturday morning when her father and I were out, she left a note saying that she was going to meet him for coffee. She said he was going to bring her some brochures from the agency. She even told us the name of the café. She said ..." Her voice broke before she uttered the last few words. "She said she would be home by noon."

"And she never came home?" Kat asked, her voice a whisper. She felt nauseated by the thought.

"*Jamais*—never. We did not see her again until her father and I went to the morgue to identify her body two years later. She had been found dead in an alley. Our beautiful Chantal, was almost unrecognizable ... All that promise, all that life ... future ... gone." Tears spilled from Élise's eyes.

"*Désolée!* Forgive me. I never know when I am going to lose control. Even though it has been more than a year since that terrible day. For two years we lived with the hope she would come back to us."

"Élise, I am so sorry," Katherine said, swallowing a lump in her throat. Her eyes met Élise's tortured gaze. "Words cannot come close to expressing my feelings."

They sat quietly together for a few minutes. Then Élise continued. "I should tell you that the police were not much help in the beginning. They said that Chantal had probably run away with a boyfriend and she would be back. A silly teenager, they suggested.

"My husband and I were the ones who phoned the modeling agency. Yes, there was a man by the name Chantal gave us and his photo matched the one she had shown us online. But he lived and worked in Paris, and he was there. He spoke to us on the phone and very indignantly told us he had nothing to do with contacting young girls online. He said we should contact the police, and he would do everything he could to help."

"And then the police became more involved?" Kat asked.

"Yes. They investigated in Paris and Nice. They went to the café with her photo. It's a big busy place and no one could recall seeing her. Then they came back to us to explain that she would be far away by now and ..."

Élise covered her face with her hands and sobbed. Katherine gave her a tissue from a pack in her pocket. She felt inadequate, helpless. "I can only imagine how difficult it is to live with the unknown," she said softly.

Élise nodded. After a few moments, she said, "Even after you know the outcome, there is so much you do not know. It never leaves you. I hope this is not the case with your friend. I would not wish this on anyone."

"I hope not too, and I thank you for taking this time with me."

"There is a support group of women, if you are interested in talking with us" Élise said. "My contact information is in our group directory. Just let me know."

There was no hesitation in the embrace the women shared now.

Katherine trembled as she returned to her seat. She thought how every single seat in the coach was taken by someone with a story. This had been a reminder that you could never tell by looking at someone what that story might be.

She was thankful that Annette was still sound asleep. There was no way she could engage in idle chatter now, and she did not want to repeat what she had just heard. She felt too drained and used the fatigue she felt after skiing all day as her reason for wanting to avoid conversation.

By now, the coach was approaching the outskirts of Nice, and traffic was slow by the airport, which was the first stop. There was backup from some remaining construction on the newly opened tramline.

Kat sat quietly, attempting to digest what she'd heard, feeling confused and distraught. Then she opened an ebook on her phone, hoping to get lost in its pages. The relaxed state of mind she had achieved on the slopes had vanished. Try as she might to concentrate, her thoughts kept slipping back to Delphine. She felt desperate for news. Desperate for good news. She checked her messages, but there were no such texts.

Annette stretched her arms as she woke. "*Mon Dieu*, that felt great. Just what I needed! Did you sleep, Kat?"

"*Un petit peu*," Katherine fibbed. "A little bit. The trip passed quickly."

After they reached the coach terminal in Nice, Katherine and Annette parted company. Kat was meeting Philippe at their favorite jazz club in the old town, just a few blocks away.

Kat had decided not to repeat to Annette the conversation with Élise. She felt drained and used fatigue as an explanation for her subdued demeanor.

"See you tomorrow at yoga," the women promised each other before they went their separate ways.

After a minute of peering through the dark interior of the jam-packed hole-in-the-wall bar, Kat spied Philippe sitting with Abdalla. The young man was the migrant from Cameroon who had saved the life of their dog Rocco. To complicate matters, he also had found a money box that a drug gang was looking for—a lucky break, as it turned out.

As an illegal migrant, normally he would have been arrested and shipped out of France. But as a witness to the discovery of the cartel's money, which then led the law enforcement people to set up a trap to arrest the guilty parties, Abdalla had to be held in protective custody until their trial. And because of that, he was now safe both from being deported and from any possible retribution from the cartel.

Philippe had arranged through Inspecteur Thibidault to take Abdalla out for an evening every two weeks. The condition they had to agree to was that the young man would wear an ankle monitor. Abdalla asked if they could go to a jazz club after they discovered they shared a passion for the music.

During his months in custody, Abdalla had shown

himself to be intelligent, interesting and determined to build a life in France. The authorities had tracked down his relatives in Paris, although he had not yet been allowed to contact them. The fact that he had family here also helped his case. It was still not known if his immediate family had perished in an attack on their village in Cameroon.

Gilles had also spent time with Abdalla, as had Véronique and David. They were all supportive of him, and all were willing to sponsor when the time finally came for his immigration hearing.

Philippe kissed Kat's cheeks as Abdalla shyly wished her *bonsoir* and offered a chair.

"The group just took a break, so your timing is perfect," Philippe said. "You don't have to talk over anything, except the buzz of conversation. I tell you, this group has enthralled everyone. There was no chatter or clatter when they were playing."

Abdalla grinned from ear to ear when Katherine asked if he was enjoying the music. "We had an awesome dinner too, *Monsieur Philippe et moi!*" he said.

"Let me guess," Kat said. "*Moules-frites?*" She knew the young man had developed a passion for the classic French dish since he had arrived.

With one look, Kat knew Philippe had seen through her attempt at levity. She leaned in and whispered, "Later. I'm okay."

Philippe put his arm around her and pulled her close, kissing her forehead. "Tell us about your Alpine exploits today. Abdalla is intrigued that it's possible to go skiing so close to Nice."

Kat was relieved to talk just about the best part of the day and enjoyed seeing the young man's eyes light up as she described Isola 2000 and all it had to offer.

"One day I hope I can go there," Abdalla said.

"One day we will make certain you do," Philippe assured him.

As soon as Kat and Philippe were alone in the car, he swept her into his arms. "*Dis-moi, Minou.* Tell me everything. Your eyes gave you away. What on earth happened?"

Philippe's embrace provided a sanctuary for Kat as she began to relate Élise's story. They remained as one until she had finished all she had to say. Philippe kissed the tears from her cheeks and held her close.

"I can imagine how difficult it was to hear that and to feel that tortured mother's pain," he said quietly.

"My heart ached for her, and of course, I couldn't stop thinking of Delphine."

———

8

*T*hursday marked a week since Kat learned that Delphine was missing. There was still no news. Life was moving on, as it does. Their first bed and breakfast guests were due today.

It was mid-afternoon when Katherine's phone pinged, indicating a text message.

"Philippe! That was Bernadette. She just left the airport with our two guests and says they will be here in a half-hour as traffic is surprisingly light along the Bord de Mer. I'm glad she's chosen that route. It means that our guests will get beautiful views of the sea and not a boring drive inland on a big highway."

Philippe joined Kat in the salon, where she had been arranging fresh flowers. He had been in the kitchen. "I've put the dogs in the laundry room and given them each a toy and their favorite elk-antler chew. That should keep them happy for a good while."

"Yes, it should. I'm so pleased we don't need to use the crates for them anymore. They've grown into such good dogs."

"*Bien sûr!* The dog run that Didier and the crew helped me build has been a godsend for Rococo now that they are older." He paused for a moment and then said, "I agree with your thoughts about Bernadette. Most taxi drivers would insist on taking the auto route. We're so fortunate she agreed to be our exclusive driver and that she is happy to bring people along the Bord de Mer road, no matter how bad the traffic is."

"The more time she has to entertain her passengers, the better she likes it."

Philippe laughed. "Well, we do know that route gives her time to spin her tales about horrible Frenchmen in her best Marseillaise accent!"

Katherine knew that this drive along the coast would leave her visitors smitten with the Côte d'Azur even before they arrived at the Villa des Violettes. It had happened to her and Molly when they first arrived from Toronto. Molly had stayed with her for the first two weeks of Kat's new life in Antibes, and the two of them had had a wonderful time exploring the town.

Bernadette had made an unforgettable impression when she picked them up that day at the airport. Kat soon learned that tight jeans, low cut colorful tops, flashy jewelry and towering stilettos were her uniform. Of indiscernible age, she changed the color of her wild, wavy hair on a regular basis. She also had become one of Kat's favorite friends.

In the time she had known her, Bernadette had proven herself to be completely reliable, honest, thoughtful, and a gifted driver. She knew the history of the French Riviera as well as the gossip, and was a born entertainer.

Kat knew that Bernadette would draw the visitors' attention to the fairytale hilltop village of Haute de Cagnes as they drove through Cagnes Sur Mer. She would regale them with the story about the discord over the building of the Baie des Anges marina and condos. Construction had begun in 1960 and took twenty-five years to complete. The iconic white buildings could be seen from a distance on land and particularly well when driving along the Bord de Mer.

After that, the road skirts a pebble beach the rest of the way to Antibes, offering the sight of sun worshippers, swimmers and people fishing, no matter the season. When the car reaches Antibes, the 500-year-old Fort Carré comes into view and the luxurious mega-yachts of Russian oligarchs and international billionaires can be seen dotting the water.

Remembering what it was like to drive this route for the first time left Katherine full of wonder at how her life had changed in one short year. This time two Septembers ago she was new to life in France, just visiting and searching for her true self. Now here she was, Madame Dufours, married to Philippe and embracing the spirit of independence she hadn't realized was part of her. Now her heart was here. Her home was here. Her family continued to grow.

Kat stepped outside through the French doors and gazed across the bay. She regularly imagined all those people, over the centuries, who had done the same thing—stopping for a moment in exactly this spot to enjoy the stunning view. A feeling of satisfaction warmed her and helped her relax a little. The truth was she and Philippe and their friends and family had brought life and laughter back to the villa, and there should always be life and laughter.

She shivered as these thoughts washed through her. There was a spirit embedded in the walls and beams and gardens of this villa that wrapped around her. Kat had never been one to believe in, or even give much thought to destiny. But now she was sure that her life at the villa was hers.

She had sensed something powerful the first time Philippe brought her here. She had seen how saddened he was by the state it was in and understood the love he had for what once had been. There had been so much they needed to do; so much they needed to know. And somehow it had all come together.

The boxes and trunks discovered in the villa's old, cobweb-filled wine cellar were filled with tattered journals and boxes of grainy, sepia photos. These treasures had offered them a glimpse of how life had been at the villa in its early years. And Simone and Oncle François had shared their priceless memories of the times they had visited the villa. Oncle François had been here often as a child, and Simone had been a regular visitor in the years after the Occupation.

Patched together, their stories had given Katherine a sense of the history of this extraordinary home. She couldn't wait to see the flowering of the violets that blanketed the entire property, for which they had chosen its new name. It wouldn't be long coming.

The new life Katherine and Philippe were creating for themselves had brought about the rebirth of the Villa des Violettes. Welcoming their first bed and breakfast guests would be the next step in its resurrection.

Kat's phone pinged again, with no message. This was the signal that Bernadette had turned up the hill toward the villa.

Kat took a quick look in the mirror, tucked her hair behind her ears, and went back to the salon. Taking

Philippe by the hand, she led him to the front doors. They looked at each other and grinned.

"*Alors, Madame Aubergiste, nous commençons!* Here we go, Madam Innkeeper!" Philippe said, and he kissed the tip of her nose.

Katherine took a deep breath, exchanged another glance with Philippe, and stepped into her new role. This adventure was on.

Bernadette pulled her van to a stop, and Philippe opened the villa's double front doors. Together they went out to greet their first guests.

A comfortably dressed couple, who appeared to be in their late sixties, smiled warmly at them. The woman had white hair, cut in a stylish bob. The man appeared fit and sported a well-worn Tilly hat. Both wore sturdy shoes and carried small backpacks. Kat smiled inwardly, thinking they looked like they had stepped out of a travel brochure for seniors.

Kat joined Philippe in greeting the guests. "*Bonjour et bienvenue, Monsieur et Madame Kingsbury.* We are happy to welcome you as the first official guests at the Villa des Violettes ... and from Canada!"

"Yes," Mrs. Kingsbury said, smiling at Katherine, "From Kingston, not far from your hometown of Toronto. We are thrilled to be here! I'm Pamela and this is my husband, Steven. It feels like we already know each other from your lovely emails."

Kat nodded. "I know Kingston well! It's a delightful town with all those historic limestone buildings."

The Kingsburys looked pleased at the recognition of their hometown.

"May we greet you in the traditional French way?" Philippe asked.

"We would be delighted to receive a French welcome."

With that Katherine and Philippe gave each of them a *bise*.

Bernadette placed the last of the luggage in the entrance hall and waved her farewells to all.

"My goodness," Pamela Kingsbury exclaimed as Bernadette drove off. "What an entertaining woman she is! I'm so glad she was waiting for us at the airport. She made everything easy."

Kat and Philippe smiled. "Bernadette is a great friend and the best taxi driver around."

Philippe took their luggage to their room, and Kat invited them to sit in the salon.

"Would you care for a cup of tea, coffee, a glass of rosé or another cold drink? How was your trip?"

The Kingsburys both said they would love a glass of wine. Philippe arrived back in time to take care of that at the sideboard, where he had earlier placed a bottle of rosé in a wine bucket. Kat slipped into the kitchen to fetch the olive board on which she had laid out some slices of saucisson and a bowl of tapenade, the standard fare.

While they were chatting, Belle sauntered in and was introduced. She was spending more time away from the kittens as they were becoming increasingly rambunctious and independent, but she never missed feeding times. Katherine told the guests they wouldn't be bothered by them as they were sequestered in the master bedroom.

"I hope we can see them at some point though," Pamela said. "We love cats, don't we, Steven?" Her husband nodded, and Kat promised a showing before they left.

Philippe asked them if he could bring Rocco and Coco in for a brief introduction. This idea was greeted with enthusiasm by the couple, who said they had a dog at home.

The dogs bounced in with their typical enthusiasm, but sat on command and calmly accepted pats on the head from the visitors.

Thank goodness for obedience school, Kat thought. *And for the ongoing care provided by sweet Delphine.* Her smile faded briefly and she fought back thoughts that would change her mood.

The weather was mild enough for the French doors to be opened briefly so that the Kingsburys could enjoy the view. Philippe took advantage of the opportunity to let the dogs have a run in the garden.

"We learned so much from your website," Steven said. "We are looking forward to exploring Antibes. It sounds intriguing."

"You will love it here," Kat said, her eyes shining. "I can assure you of that. Let us know if you have any questions."

As she led the Kingsburys down the hall, she pointed to the side door in the kitchen. "That will be your entrance to the house when we are not home. There is a combination lock on the door and the numbers are on an information sheet in your room. There is also a cell phone in there to use locally, and we can text each other using that. We will always let you know if we will be out."

Then Katherine showed the guests to their room and pointed out the brochures and printouts of local information she had left for them on the desk between the French doors.

She smiled when they exclaimed at the size of the key for the lock on their bedroom door, remembering the enormous key she had been given when she first arrived in Antibes for her home exchange with the Browns. She had loved holding that key, and opening the door with it had given her a thrill.

After a few words of explanation about where things were in the part of the house that was open to guests, Katherine left them to make their own plans.

"If you wish to go into the old town this evening, you can easily walk. Otherwise we can arrange for Bernadette to pick you up at whatever time you like. You can let her know where to collect you when you are ready to come back."

The couple had a few questions and then indicated they were happy to unpack and get settled before they made any other plans. "We are planning to go into the old town for dinner but we are going to walk. Thank you for your recommendations."

"*D'accord*! We will see you for breakfast tomorrow."

9

"*A*re you almost ready to leave for Simone's? We are supposed to be there at seven-thirty, *non*?" Philippe called down the hall to Katherine, who was changing in their bedroom.

"*C'est vrai!* Exactly! I'm almost finished. I got a little side-tracked playing with the kittens. They are becoming so cute. I just have to put on my mascara. You know I can't go out the door without it!"

Philippe smiled. He knew that was his wife's one obsession with her beauty regimen. He thought she looked just fine without it, but she was not to be deterred. In a few seconds she said she was ready.

Simone had invited Didier and his crew, as well as Kat and Philippe, for a special meal. She had taken the work crew under her wing in the past year, since they were far away from their homes in the Pays Basque. Today she had told them she was preparing a classic French meal, pot-au-feu.

"You know by now it's the quintessence of family cuisine

in France," Philippe said to Kat as they walked along the path to Simone's.

"I remember when Simone made it for us last year. It was delicious. She said then that every good French mother would prepare this for her family on special occasions. Now I'm feeling a little guilty that I haven't done so yet," Kat said. "But only a little. I'll get around to it one of these days."

"Absolutely no rush. I have no complaints about the quality of our cuisine, and I particularly like that you are happy to have me in there preparing meals with you."

"*J'adore ça!* I love that you like to cook too. You know that." Kat flashed him a wide grin.

When they arrived at Simone's, Kat tapped the brass knocker on the front door and they walked in, as was their custom. Otherwise, Simone would keep the door locked and would have to leave her studio or the kitchen to unlock it and let them in. It had taken some time for them to convince Simone to leave it unlocked for them and save herself the journey, but eventually she had grudgingly conceded that times had changed and she needed to conserve her energy.

The ambiance could not have been more funereal. The house was silent, and for a moment Kat wondered where everyone was. Then, one after another, the men came from the salon to greet Kat and Philippe in the foyer. Each of them in turn asked about Delphine and expressed his sorrow that she was missing. It was obvious that Alfonso was particularly heartbroken. His voice broke as he spoke her name.

Normally, their meals at Simone's began with a bottle of champagne. "This evening will be no different," Simone decreed, once they were all seated in the salon. "We will sip our champagne and honor our Delphine. We will toast to her safe return." And so they did.

A hearty aroma wafted out from the kitchen. Kat could see the large cast-iron pot in which the classic beef stew was simmering, and she knew that it would include carrots, turnips, leeks, celery, and onions studded with cloves. Simone would have made her own *bouquet garni*, a tied bundle of sage, bay leaves, and thyme, to add to the pot.

Simone graciously accepted Kat's offer of help, and said to Philippe, " I have a task for you too, just like your dear *maman* would have had."

"Your timing is perfect," Simone said as she removed the onion from the pot. Without needing to be told, Philippe transferred the meat and vegetables to a large heated platter. The last time Simone made this dish he had explained to Kat that this had been his task in his mother's kitchen.

Katherine followed instructions to pour the broth through a sieve into a warm pot. At the table, it would be ladled into small bowls and served as soup. In the meantime, Philippe removed the marrow from the bones and spread it on small toasts. "Mmmm, *quel délice!* The special treat we eat first. We kids would fight over this," he said

When the meal had been placed on the table, Simone rang the dinner bell.

"Now please, let us all join hands," Simone said, once they were all seated. She bowed her head, and the others followed her example. "We gather here as Delphine's loved ones, her family. It is essential that we continue to believe that she will be returned to us safely. We don't know where she is or why she is gone, but we hold in our hearts the hope that the spirits of the universe will watch over her and return her safely home."

All four men were distressed that someone they cared for had disappeared, but none more than Alfonso. At the Christmas meal they had shared at Kat and Philippe's, it had been obvious to Kat that Alfonso's dark, dreamy eyes had followed Delphine's every move. She had been certain love was in the air. Now she sensed that more than ever.

Kat was touched to hear how all four men had distributed flyers about Delphine and searched for some sort of answer. Alfonso and Alesandro had driven up into the hills of the *arrière-pays* and stopped to post flyers in every hamlet, village, and town along the way.

"We will go again this weekend and cover as much territory as possible," Alfonso pledged. His voice was thick with emotion.

Philippe expressed his frustration at not hearing anything from the police. However, Inspector Thibidault had warned him this was the way such investigations were handled. "He explained in great detail the complexities of these cases. There is always involvement on many levels, local and national."

As they ate and conversed, Kat contemplated how the unlikely group around the table had become her new family.

First, of course, was Philippe. Her husband, lover, and partner of almost one year. A time that had outshone her previous twenty-two year unhappy marriage in every way.

Ninety-five-year-old Simone, a true matriarch, had taken a place in Kat's heart on the day they first met. Her donkey's persistent braying had made Kat follow him to the house where she found that Simone had accidentally locked herself in her studio.

Didier was the chief contractor for the restoration of the villa. He was short and stocky with bulging muscles and a creative genius with wood, stone and structures. He was also a proud native of the elegant seaside town of Biarritz in the historic Pays Basque. The one quirk of his personality was his insistence on wearing a beret at all times, even under a hardhat when he was on the job. He swore it was the best hat for all weather conditions. He was thirty-one and had never married, but his gruff exterior hid a heart of gold.

Alesandro and Alfonso were brothers, a year apart in age, from a small town outside Biarritz. They were Didier's cousins, a few years younger than he and true romantics. Tall with olive complexions and deep dark eyes. They were charming and shy, and loved to quote poetry and sing as they put all their effort into whatever task Didier assigned them.

From Calais, Auguste was also one of Didier's cousins. His mother was the only member of Didier's family to leave the Pays Basque, but she had made certain Auguste never forgot his roots. In his mid-thirties, he was the biggest man Kat had ever seen and, with great affection, she called him "the gentle giant." He worked quickly and nimbly in spite of his size. His first love was gardening and nurturing anything to grow. He had spent many evenings working on the villa's flower beds, helping to bring them to life again.

Kat had long ago learned that listening to the four men converse in the Basque language, Euskara, was entertaining even though she could not understand what they said. They would often burst into *bertsolari* duels, typical of the region, where a team of two people compete with others in singing an improvised poem set to a classic Basque tune.

"We're manipulating words and melody and trying to outdo each other," Alesandro had explained, as they translated for each other to the rest of the room. Fits of laughter and good-natured ribbing were an integral part of the competition.

The one person who was missing at the table was Delphine. Over the previous year, she too had become part of Kat's family. Her loving nature and considerate acts, and the question of what had happened to her dominated the conversation throughout the meal. Everyone felt helpless about her disappearance.

The men cleared the table and washed the dishes. The Basque contingent had already established this tradition whenever the group ate together, and this evening Philippe joined them. Kat and Simone watched them, singing while they worked and teasing each other. It struck Kat that the simple act of washing and drying dishes nearly always brought people together.

After the last dish was dried and put away, Didier and his crew of cousins left. Philippe and Kat got up to leave too, but Simone asked them to remain behind as she had something to discuss. The three of them sat at the kitchen table, where so many good conversations happened.

"I've been thinking about this a great deal," Simone began, looking into their eyes in turn. "All of this talk about family tonight has brought it to the forefront of my thoughts. So I have a request to make of you when you visit Corsica in April."

"No request from you would ever be an issue," Philippe said, and Kat nodded in agreement.

Simone continued. "As you know, I stole away from Paris to my aunt's in Corsica after the war, to give birth to my son, Jean-Luc. I was also hiding from my lover, your grandfather, Gregoire Dufours. In spite of the wrench of thinking our love affair was over, those were some of the most peaceful days of my life." She looked at Philippe as she spoke. He nodded his understanding. Simone had talked to him and Kat the year before about this history, and it had lodged deeply in his heart. Particularly when it became clear that he and Jean-Luc were related by blood. They were family.

Katherine felt her face flush as she recalled that conversation Simone had with her and Philippe in that very room, almost a year before.

The three of them had been sitting in the same places as they were at this moment. Simone had spoken then of her years in Corsica and the return of her lover, Gregoire, with unabated passion. She and Gregoire, a married man, had worked in the Resistance together and had fallen in love. At the end of the war, when she realized she was pregnant, Simone had insisted he return to his wife and children and then had stolen away to Corsica. A year later, Gregoire tracked her down and walked back into her life, delighted to discover the son he had not known existed.

Simone had painted evocative pictures of their time together, talking about the long walks they took through the hills, making love in fields of flowers while Jean-Luc napped peacefully next to them. Kat recalled watching Simone transform from a woman of ninety-five years back into her younger self at these memories. She could see the same softening of Simone's features now. Her eyes were bright and she leaned forward, drawing them both under her spell.

Kat could recall verbatim Simone's powerful message from another memorable evening, when Philippe had placed a stunning pink diamond engagement ring on Katherine's finger. "No matter what obstacle or heartbreak is put in our paths, we alone choose to be happy. No one else makes that choice for us." Simone's words held even more meaning for Kat than she might have imagined.

Now Simone said, "I know I don't need to repeat the story about my time in Corsica to you. But I was thinking about it this week as I grieved for Delphine, and it brought me to this decision and the request I am about to make."

"*Je t'assure, Cherie Simone*, no request would be too

much," Philippe repeated. His love for Simone was anchored deeply in his heart. Only more so when she revealed that her lover was his grandfather.

"*C'est interessant*," Simone said, "why we have intentions that we sometimes never act upon. This is one. I have never returned to Corsica, to that place of such love, peace and passion just a few hours away. *Jamais!* I cannot tell you why."

Katherine and Philippe sat quietly, and he slipped Kat's hand into his. Both of them could feel the intensity of Simone's emotions as she spoke.

"I have saved a small urn of Jean-Luc's ashes. If possible, it would put this old mother's heart at peace to know they have been returned to that place so dear to us—*ceux qui nous sont chers.*"

"Of course."

"*Bien sûr.*"

Kat and Philippe answered at the same time.

"This will be a priority, and we will carry out your wishes with great love," Philippe said.

10

*A*s they walked hand in hand back to the villa, Kat said, "This is not the first time that Simone has helped remind me that everyone has a story, no matter their age. Just because a person no longer looks young, does not mean they do not feel love just as intensely as they once did."

"C'est vrai," Philippe said.

"I could feel her passion this evening." Kat spoke softly, her voice still affected by the ardor Simone's words had stirred in her. She moved his arm from her waist to around her shoulders and pressed her body to his.

Philippe stopped, and they stood in the moonlight, kissing with sweet tenderness. He ran his fingers through her hair, as their lips met again and again. "Let's go straight to our room," he whispered in her ear.

Kat felt the familiar irresistible desire for Philippe, but then reality broke the spell.

"But first, *mon amour*, we have to let the dogs out. And, who knows, our houseguests may be waiting up to chat with us."

"*Les chiens, oui!* The dogs must go out. But the guests? They don't have access to us now, *non*?" Philippe asked.

"Not really, but we have to go into the kitchen to get the dogs. The guests may be at the table, having a late night snack. I told them they could," Kat said.

"Hmm. We will have to reorganize that," Philippe said.

Kat nodded. "Yes, I didn't think that part through very well. We can leave the dogs in the salon next time."

At the front door, Katherine stopped to look at the wisteria vine where it was illuminated by lamplight. "It's going to be so beautiful when it's in bloom. I can't wait for spring to fully arrive!"

Philippe agreed and hastily pulled her inside. "Let's get those dogs out. I can't wait for holding you in my arms to arrive!"

Kat laughed and put a finger to her lips. "Our guests!"

Philippe shook his head and raised his eyebrows. "That's not going to happen."

They entered the kitchen hesitantly. There was no sign of life but a note on the counter read, "We had a wonderful evening in the old town. Thank you for the excellent restaurant recommendation! See you at breakfast. Pamela and Steven."

Philippe fist pumped and he opened the door to the mudroom. The dogs tumbled out joyfully. Kat was pleased they didn't bark. Their training was coming along well. Which, of course, made her think of Delphine. Philippe noticed the change in her expression and asked what the matter was.

"Oh *Chouchou*," she said, "my mind just raced back to Delphine. After all of our talk this evening, I was starting to feel positive that she's safe and will come back. Seeing the dogs has made me fearful for her again."

Philippe took her hand and gently pulled her outside with the dogs. As Coco and Rocco raced down to the stone wall to find their favorite place to squat, Philippe embraced Kat on the terrace.

"Put your face to the moonlight *mon coeur ... ma belle*! And hold that positive thought about Delphine. We must keep believing. I am determined to do just that."

Kat repeated his words. "Keep believing, yes. So many people have told me they are lighting candles and praying for her."

"Everything is being done that can be done."

Coco and Rocco soon raced back for their treats and then scampered down to the master bedroom. After a few minutes of petting and snuggling with the dogs, Kat and Philippe prepared to go to bed. It had been a busy day.

"There are times when we need to put aside everything else, *Minou*. This is one of them. Come to me," he tenderly invited, taking her in his arms. "Let's just be us for now."

---

11

*T*he morning sun was fast drying the dew on the grass as the dogs dashed about. Kat strolled along the perennial borders looking at all the green shoots poking up through the soil. From what she could see, there soon would be a magnificent array of spring flowers.

All winter, Auguste had worked hard at clearing and reorganizing these vast flowerbeds. The preliminary work had been accomplished the previous spring before Kat and Philippe's wedding reception in the garden. This winter, he had tackled the back garden.

Kat let her memories take her back to that unforgettable day she and Philippe were married at the Mairie. The garden reception had been a surprise planned by Philippe and their daughter, Adorée, with the help of their friends. It had been a dream come true—a celebration of love and joy in its purest form. Everyone who meant something to her had been there, thanks to their friend, Nick, who flew her Toronto family and friends over in a private jet. Everyone had been there, including Delphine. Kat sighed loudly.

The dogs ran up from the stone wall and bounced around her. Her thoughts flashed to Delphine. She had fallen in love with the pups partly because of Delphine's deep affection for them and how they responded to her. Watching her handle the pups had shown Kat a side of the young woman that her Goth appearance disguised.

It was now nine days since Delphine had left the refuge. Nothing could keep thoughts of her from occupying Kat's mind for long.

"Where are you, Delphine?" Kat said out loud, looking out across the bay. "Where are you? I hope you are safe."

After calling the dogs back to the villa, Kat went inside. She had a plan for the day.

She had emailed Élise Fortier, the woman on the bus who had shared her daughter's shocking story. This afternoon she was going to meet her in Nice and attend a meeting of the mothers' group Élise had mentioned. Kat hoped to learn more about human trafficking, and perhaps discover a reason why Delphine had left the refuge so abruptly.

With Philippe already at the market, Katherine began to prepare breakfast for the Kingsburys. Eight a.m. was the posted time for guests to be in the breakfast room. Simone's fresh madeleines were already sitting in a basket on the kitchen island, next to a box of patisseries delivered as promised by one of Didier's team.

As she set the table, Kat congratulated herself for the way they had designed this area. A compact, bright space had been created to one side of the kitchen, and furnished with two tables that could be set for two or four people or joined together for a group of eight. Two sets of French doors led to a sheltered terrace where their guests could dine *al fresco* when the weather permitted.

Promptly at 8:00, Pamela and Stephen Kingsbury appeared, looking eager to start their day.

"Bonjour! Did you sleep well?" Kat greeted them.

"We did indeed, thank you," Pamela said with a warm smile. "Our room is so quiet, and the bed as comfortable as can be." Her husband nodded in agreement and added, "We're excited to get on with our day."

A part of Katherine's regimen for running the inn was asking guests to fill out a breakfast questionnaire posted on the villa's website before they arrived. In this way, she knew what to prepare for the morning. A French press of fresh coffee was already on the table, along with a still-warm baguette and a selection of fruit jams. Now Kat brought the madeleines and a basket of croissants, pain au chocolat and pain aux raisins.

"This is a classic French breakfast, as I'm sure you know," Kat said as she put them down. "The madeleines are a treat from our ninety-five-year-old neighbor."

She returned to the kitchen to fetch a bowl of fresh fruit salad and a plate arrayed with soft boiled eggs, sausages and sliced ham. None of these were at all typical of a French breakfast, but it was what the Kingsburys had requested.

"This is perfect," Pamela said.

Katherine smiled to herself, pleased that her idea of the questionnaire was working.

"Enjoy your breakfast. I will be in the next room taking care of a few things, so call me if you need anything at all. *Bon appétit!*"

A short while later, Katherine heard her name being called and joined her guests in the breakfast area. They thanked her effusively for the meal and said they had some questions to ask about the day they had planned. Kat suspected this would be her favorite part of running an inn.

There were few things she enjoyed more than sharing her knowledge and love of the area.

After a short chat about their itinerary, Steven excused himself to go to their room. Pamela remained with Kat and shuffled nervously for a moment. Then she cleared her throat and spoke with some hesitation, as tears pooled in her eyes. "I thought I should let you know that Steven was diagnosed with Alzheimer's early last year."

Kat was surprised and her heart went out to her guest. "I'm so sorry, Pamela. This must have been difficult news for you both to absorb."

"Yes, it took us a while to come to terms with it." Pamela blinked rapidly and recovered her composure. "But now we are doing everything we can to move forward positively. We recognized that travel might become difficult in the future so we planned this trip."

"What a fine idea," Kat murmured.

Pamela continued. "Steven and I met on the beach in Juan-les-Pins back in the sixties, and then we camped at various sites along the coast for a few weeks that summer. It was a time when all of our friends—all of us were footloose and fancy-free—were traveling around Europe. Most of us had just finished university and wanted a fling before settling down to find a job. What a time!"

"I can imagine," Kat said. "What memories you must have!"

"For sure! We always planned to come back, but you know how things go in life: careers, family, and the next thing we know, we are old! So we thought this would be a good trip to make while Steve can still recall what happened in the places we visited. The first thing we would like to do is walk some of the hiking trails—they're called *sentiers*, right? We brought maps with us."

Katherine smiled. "You can easily walk from here to *le Sentier du Littoral*, which goes around Cap d'Antibes. The trail will only take an hour or so to walk, but there are many places to stop and enjoy the view. If you wish, you can keep going and walk to Juan-les-Pins. I will give you Bernadette's number, so that she can collect you and bring you back here. How does that sound?"

"That sounds perfect," Pamela replied, her eyes shining with excitement. "We can have lunch in Juan-les-Pins and look for the beach where we met."

"You will see that things have changed quite dramatically, but I'm sure you will find that special spot" Kat said with a grin. "There are bottles of water in the fridge. Please take a few with you for the walk. And don't forget sunscreen."

"This is wonderful. Yes, we have sunscreen with us," Pamela assured her. "Thank you so much."

"One more thing," Kat said. "We have hired a young student to clean the bathrooms and make the beds for guests in the morning. If you would rather not have anyone go in your room, just let us know. Lucille will be here doing other housework for us and also studying, as she attends classes in the late afternoon and evening. You can call her on the phone we left you, if you have a problem, and she can reach us."

Lucille was the daughter of one of the flower vendors in the market, and when Philippe heard she was looking for a few hours of part-time work, he had spoken with Kat about hiring her. They had decided it was important for Kat to have time for photography rather than spend it cleaning, and Lucille was happy to take the job. The workload would be light at first, but as more guests came, the hours would be better for her.

"That would be lovely, thank you," Pamela said. "We will be off shortly."

atherine caught the 1:20 p.m. train to Nice and arrived twenty minutes later. It was a short walk to her rendezvous, through one of the more beautiful quarters of the town. Normally, the stunning architecture of the buildings would completely absorb her and her camera. Not so today. There was only one thing on her mind—how she and those around her had suddenly found themselves dragged into thinking about the world of human trafficking.

We don't even know for certain that this is what has happened to Delphine. Are we simply speculating? Over-reacting? We're just going on what Raymond Albert said Delphine told him, but what else can we do? As arranged, Élise Fortier was waiting for Katherine at a table in the quirky modern-art filled interior of the Scotch Tea House. She appeared even more petite and fragile than Kat remembered her being on the bus ride from Isola 2000.

"This is such a good place to meet with others," Kat said. "When I first came to Nice, I assumed from its name that this was where all the Anglophones gathered. I soon learned it was popular with locals too."

"*Tout à fait*," Élise agreed. "The lunches and desserts are excellent. What really works for our group is that they have a lovely meeting room in the back, which we get to use at no expense. We have time for a cup of tea or coffee before the others arrive. What would you like?"

Thirty women attended the meeting—grandmothers, mothers, sisters and friends of victims of the sex trade came to share their stories and to support each other. To Kat's surprise, there were also a few girls who, like Delphine, had managed to escape their horrific circumstances. By the time the meeting ended two hours later, Katherine felt emotionally wrung out. She had heard stories of anguishing situations she had previously only read about or heard reported in news broadcasts and had been shocked to hear the statistics on missing girls and women in France. Some of the stories ended well and others did not. Many were ongoing nightmares. Everyone at the meeting was deeply affected by what they heard, and feelings of anger, disgust, fear, sorrow and hope all mixed together within the confines of the room. Tears were shed. The stories made the horror of human trafficking so much more substantive—and painful.

There was much discussion about how to educate the general public. Katherine felt hopeful learning about the volunteer organizations throughout the country that were staffed by people trained in crisis intervention and communication. A nation-wide data base had also been set up. Still, the disappearances were difficult to track, and it was becoming even harder to find the missing girls.

"We often have many more people here ... sometimes men too," Elise told Kat. "Our group is a bit separate from the association that looks into women and girls from outside the country who are trafficked here. Our primary focus is on our own, French girls."

Kat added her name to a list of people willing to volunteer and was told someone would be in touch with her. Her thoughts swirled madly all the way as she returned to Antibes on the train. She had no idea what she could do. All she knew was that she wanted to try to help in some way.

"We can never have enough people taking up this cause, Madame Dufours," Élise told her.

By 6:00 p.m., Katherine was in the kitchen preparing a small bowl of tapenade to go with the fresh baguette she had picked up on her walk back from the train station. Philippe was pouring pastis. It was *l'heure de l'apéro*. Cocktail hour.

Kat could not stop talking about the meeting.

"*Minou*, I understand how difficult it must have been for you to hear all of that," Philippe said. "But I'm glad you went. We must see what we can do within our own community."

"I was thinking about Delphine the whole time. She's the reason I was there. My heart is aching at the thought that she has been forced back into the sex trade. Can you try to find out something from the police tomorrow?"

Philippe promised to try.

The dogs barked briefly as Pamela and Steven came through the front door. Kat said, "Okay. I'm going to put on my cheery innkeeper face and set this afternoon aside for now. Not that it will be easy."

She went to greet them. "How was your day of hiking?"

Husband and wife flashed two thumbs up, and Pamela offered a flurry of superlatives. "It couldn't have been better," she said with a grin. "Thank you for your advice."

"Would you like to join us for an *apéro*?" Kat asked, as Philippe came into the salon carrying a tray with drinks and *petits goûts*.

Steven mumbled a "no thank you" and rushed past them to their room.

"Please excuse him," Pamela apologized. "He's exhausted. But we did have a wonderful day. We walked all the way to Juan-les-Pins, as you suggested. And we found our special beach! Imagine! Steven spotted it almost immediately, in spite of all the development that has gone on through the years. Then we had a late and delicious lunch overlooking the bay."

"Considering the fact that you probably both are jet-lagged, I'd say you accomplished a lot today! Are you planning to go out for dinner?"

"Jet lag is definitely getting the best of us now. We will pass on dinner tonight. We picked up a baguette sandwich to share on the terrace later, if that's okay."

"Of course," Kat and Philippe both said at the same time.

Pamela continued, "But I will join you for a glass of wine now. Thank you!"

Sitting in the salon, with the French doors open, they watched the setting sun turn the sky into swirls of every shade of pink.

When Pamela mentioned some of the other places she and Steven hoped to visit, Kat offered an idea. "Why not see if you can book Bernadette for a day and give her your itinerary? It will make visiting those places much more enjoyable and less tiring for you and Steven. You won't have to worry about traffic and parking. You can both sit back and enjoy the wonderful scenery."

"That's a brilliant idea. I think we'll do just that. We may be able to work in a hike or two when we go up into the hills. Bernadette can drop us off and meet us at the other end," Pamela said. "I'm getting excited already!"

"Do you hike a lot at home in Canada?" Philippe asked.

Nodding, Pamela told them, "We have always been avid hikers, even when our children were young. And I thank goodness that Steven loves to do it, because walking is a major help with Alzheimer's. You would think that he would never even be a candidate for the disease after all we've done!"

"It must be frustrating. Especially when you think you've done everything right," Kat said.

Pamela's shoulders sagged and her expression registered her disappointment. "And we've also been lifelong ballroom dancers. Double insurance, you might guess. But, nope." She threw her arms up in frustration.

"Some things in life simply can't be predicted or explained, right?" Katherine said sympathetically, her thoughts drifting to Delphine again.

"Absolutely not," Pamela said. Lifting her wine glass, she added, "So let's raise our glasses in a toast to good health and to living a life with no regrets."

"*Santé*," Philippe offered. "To good health."

"Nothing better," Pamela said, and they all agreed.

13

The next few days passed quickly. Kat immersed herself in her role as innkeeper, making notes about the reality of having guests—who really were strangers—in her home. She was thankful Philippe had suggested they begin with just two guests. That had been a smart move and she was learning much from their stay.

Pamela and Steven had booked in for six days and were going to England afterward to visit Steven's birthplace. They were ideal guests who spent most of the day away. Otherwise they appeared happy to be in their room or sitting on their terrace reading when they were at the villa. Katherine only saw them for breakfast each morning and Pamela, on her own, for the occasional *apéro*.

"Lucille is a godsend. When she's finished cleaning, she's going to stay here and study for the rest of the day, so we don't need to hurry home," Kat told Philippe on Saturday afternoon before they roared off on his motorcycle. "There are so many aspects of running a B&B that I simply did not think of until it was actually happening."

Philippe agreed. *"Ce n'était qu'un essai.* We took a test, *non?"*

Kat smiled, knowing he was teasing her again with his translation. "Yes, it was a test run. I'm starting to see the challenges that may occur when we have more than two guests in a few weeks."

As he revved the motor and rubbed his hands lovingly over the handlebars of his vintage Ducati motorcycle, Philippe said, "Let's talk about it later. For now, we will try to forget about everything else for a few hours. We have to get in shape for touring Corsica on this old girl! We haven't been out on her enough these last few months. Where would you like to go today?"

"Let's head up to Les Tourrettes," Kat suggested. It had been their destination on their first ride together on the motorcycle, and the first time Katherine had let down her inhibitions and felt the full force of her physical attraction to Philippe. It was the beginning of the love affair that led to the lifelong commitment they made at their wedding eight months later.

Philippe had driven the roads that lead up into the *arrière-pays* for his entire adult life. He had a passion for them, as well as for his vintage Ducati, which he handled like a maestro. It smoothly put the distance behind them, climbing the winding roads and hugging the switchback corners. All along the route, panoramic vistas suddenly burst into view. At times, they gazed across dense forests and mountain gorges, some with sparkling waterfalls. Other times, the view stretched south to the glittering sea. Katherine exclaimed joyfully at each new sight.

"I never tire of these views," she murmured into her headset, which carried her message to his ears. Pressed against his back, she nuzzled his neck and breathed in the smell of him, which still made the back of her legs tingle, just like that first time—a time she was certain she would never forget.

Whenever it was safe to pull off the narrow road, Philippe stopped, if asked, so Kat could hop off and take a few photos.

They passed several villages either set off the road or perched above them, but, after crossing a bridge over the river, the road they were on ran right through the hamlet of Pont du Loup.

"Time for a quick coffee," Philippe suggested.

They were soon seated on the terrace of the only café open.

"Everything here will soon be back in business when hiking begins in earnest next month. The waterfalls should be quite impressive this spring with the runoff from all the snow higher up," Philippe said. "Did you know that Queen Victoria used to take the train up here when she was in residence on the Riviera? This area was quite a fashionable tourist destination in Victorian times."

Kat smiled. No matter where they went, Philippe always had, at the very least, some historical detail to share. Often there was a lengthy story attached, and Kat loved to hear the history of all of these interesting places. It brought them to life for her.

"I always feel a twinge of sadness when we ride past what is left of the railway bridge back there," Kat told him as she sipped her café au lait. "The remains of its majestic arches have a forlorn air about them. My reaction is probably partly due to knowing they were blown up by the

Germans during the Occupation in 1944. They are a tragic reminder of those terrible times."

Philippe patted her hand. "And yet the world moves on. Imagine how many thousands of people drive by those ruins every year with no idea of their history. Shall we get going?"

He left their payment in the small dish that held their bill—the efficient way this was done in France.

Katherine stared intently past Philippe. Her attention had been seized by a commotion in a parking lot on the other side of the narrow road and up a bit from the café. Two men were shoving each other, and a woman with long blond hair was trying to keep them apart. They were all yelling angrily.

Kat sputtered, "Isn't ... isn't ... that the nasty looking fellow we saw at Carnaval when we caught a glimpse of Delphine and you took off after them?"

"*Mon Dieu!*" Philippe gulped. "I think you are right."

The woman had turned to face the terrace where they were sitting and was shaking her head and gesticulating wildly. She was shouting at the men, although Kat couldn't make out her words.

Kat gasped. "That's Delphine! I'm sure of it. I'd recognize her mannerisms anywhere!"

She began to get up from the table, but Philippe grabbed her arm. "*Fais attention, Minou!* You don't know anything for sure, and it looks like those men are going to fight. Who knows what is going on? And how can that possibly be Delphine?"

"She's wearing a wig! I know it's her! I'm telling you—" Kat's voice rose.

"Shhh! Whatever you do, do not call out!" Philippe

warned. "They look like a rough crowd! Who knows how they would react to our getting involved!"

Kat picked up her backpack to take out her camera. "If I can't go over there, I'm taking a photo. I can zoom in with my lens."

The three people were all shouting, with the occasional shove, engrossed in their altercation. They were paying attention to nothing else. Kat moved to a nearby tree to be less conspicuous, and Philippe followed her.

"Look through the lens," she hissed at him, her voice harsh with anxiety. "I'm telling you that's Delphine! Call your contact at the police department. We have to do something!"

Philippe looked doubtful but he pulled out his cell phone and tapped in a number. He was on the phone when a white van screeched into the parking lot. A man jumped out of the vehicle and joined the fray for a minute. Then they all climbed into the van, still shouting at one other.

Kat heard Philippe leave a message. Voicemail! She grabbed his arm roughly. "We can't wait for them to get back to you! We have to follow them."

Philippe reluctantly agreed, and they were back on the road in no time, following the van at a safe distance. The succession of tight bends in the road caused them to lose sight of it occasionally, but there were no roads or lanes leading off that the van might have taken.

"*Merde!* That driver has his foot to the floor!" Philippe remarked.

A few minutes later, a black car with darkened windows careened past them at top speed, almost forcing them off the road.

Kat hung on for all she was worth, gasping for breath. But she had every confidence in Philippe's ability to maintain control. She remembered the time in Entrevaux when a similar type of chase had happened and she had thought it was going to be the end of them.

Farther up, the road straightened for a stretch. In the distance, they could see construction workers in bright yellow vests, digging at the side of the road. They watched the van go past the three workers and make a sharp right turn up a lane, followed closely by the black car. As they drew closer, the construction workers placed barriers across the road, before the turn to the lane, and put up a stop sign.

One man held up his hand and shouted at them to stop. "*Arrêt! Vous ne pouvez pas passer!*" Another drove a small digger onto the road, and the third began to shovel dirt in the ditch. Their efforts were not convincing.

"*Qu'est-ce qui ce passe ici?* What's going on?" Philippe demanded, after bringing the bike to a stop.

The man who appeared to be in charge gave a long-winded explanation why the road was closed temporarily that made no sense to Kat.

Suddenly the sounds of gunshots rang out. All the construction men dove to the ground. Philippe grabbed Kat and pulled her down behind the Ducati.

Their hearts pounding, they whispered to each other.

"We need to get out of here!" Philippe said.

"But what if that is Delphine in there? We need to help her!" Kat hissed.

"We don't know who is there or what is happening, but gunshots are never good news. We need to leave now!"

Now they could hear the distinctive two-note sounds of police sirens coming closer, and the men quickly moved their construction barriers aside. Two police vans raced past them and up the lane. The men put the barriers back just as quickly and stood in the road, glaring at Kat and Philippe, as they picked themselves up from behind the bike.

"What is going on?" Philippe asked again, his voice filled with urgency.

Kat was beside herself with anxiety and ran up to them, yelling in a mix of French and English, "We know the young woman in the van. She's our friend, and she's been missing for over a week. It was her! We need to help her!"

The lead worker pulled out a police badge. "*Désolé, c'est une affaire pour la police. Vous devez partir. Maintenant!*" Adding in broken English, "It's just for the police. You must to go now!"

After talking in a calmer voice failed to persuade the officer to let them through, Philippe said to Kat, "We will not learn anything else here. He's telling us to go back—in no uncertain terms!"

"But ... but ...," Kat sputtered. Her face was completely drained of color. "We can't just go home. I won't be able to think straight until we know what is going on here. I'm sure it was Delphine that we saw, and I want to know whether she is safe. We have to stay!"

Philippe hugged and tried to calm her. "I know you're certain it's Delphine. But we know nothing for sure. We will just have to wait and hope, but not here. We absolutely cannot stay. The officer says there is another roadblock farther on as well. He said we have to get out of here or we will be arrested."

Kat was so frustrated she couldn't speak. She shuffled her feet, her hands clenched. "We have to do something!"

Philippe picked up the bike and climbed on, telling Kat to do the same. "I will call the police in Nice as soon as we get home. But we have to leave now."

Kat reluctantly got on behind him, almost crying with

disappointment. Philippe drove the bike slowly back down the road toward Antibes. At one of their favorite viewing spots, he pulled over and parked. He led her to the rocky ledge from where they could see red-tiled rooftops dotting the hills that tumbled down to the sea.

They sat side by side, Kat's hand nestled in Philippe's. For a long time, they said nothing. Then Philippe took a deep breath and began. "*Mon amour*, I know you think the woman was Delphine, but I don't want you to be disappointed again. You've been filled with hope before, only to have those hopes dashed."

Kat looked down at her hands. "*Tu as raison*. You are right," she said softly. "I might have let my imagination carry me away. But, honestly, I felt sure it was Delphine—her body language; the way she was moving her hands—I wanted so badly for it to be her. I don't want to give up hope that she will come back to us."

"I'm not saying to give up," Philippe said. "But I am saying that today may have been about something else entirely. It may have had nothing to do with Delphine. We don't know what happened back there, and we need to let it go."

They remained on the ledge, watching shades of pink and gold paint the sky as the sun set. Katherine felt tears trickle down her cheeks before she lost control and wept.

"There is so much beauty in this world. So much to make us happy ..." Her voice was cracking with emotion, "Why does there have to be evil that pushes goodness aside and ... why someone like Delphine, who has suffered so much already?" Sobs racked her body, and she covered her face with her hands.

Philippe held her in his arms and gently rocked her. "Get it out, *Minou*. Try to let go of what is hurting you."

In time, Kat became calmer. After several long sighs, she kissed Philippe on the cheek. "Thank you for being so patient with me."

Philippe brushed Kat's forehead with his lips. "Now, don't miss this stunning sunset. Get your camera out."

Katherine took her time composing images, allowing the peace that photography always brought her to work its spell. But her heart remained heavy with sorrow, and she scolded herself. She knew Philippe was right and that she had to stop obsessing about Delphine. *I am not going to give up hope,* she thought, *but I am going to try to focus on the positive things in life instead of imagining what has happened to her.*

"It's fun being back on the bike, *Chouchou*," Katherine said, trying to lighten her mood. "Even if our ride hasn't exactly turned out as we planned."

Philippe snorted. "*C'est peu dire!*"

"To say the least, is right. The whole situation is surreal."

"Let's go home, make dinner and find something new to watch on Netflix. We've finished that last series."

"I'm going to fill the tub to the brim and have a good long soak first," Kat said. "Something tells me I'm going to need it."

14

*A*fter breakfast on Tuesday, Pamela and Steven said goodbye to Kat. Philippe had already left for an early morning meeting at the market.

"We loved staying here and can't thank you enough for all your help and advice," Pamela said. "And Bernadette! We would never have discovered her without you. You all made our visit to the Côte d'Azur more special than we had thought possible." Steven nodded and quietly voiced his thanks.

Katherine was sorry to see them go. "Thank you for your patience. As our first guests, we learned from having you here. And thank you for sharing your story with us. We won't forget it."

She handed Pamela a small paper bag tied with a lavender ribbon. "Here are some madeleines to take on the next part of your journey."

Steven unexpectedly spoke up. "Those were the best ever! Thank you. And we loved the dogs and all the kittens too." His face lit up with a grin. Pamela nodded, "We had a visit with at least one of the kittens every evening."

Katherine grinned at that just as her phone pinged with a text from Bernadette. She was almost there to take the Kingsburys to the train station.

Lucille helped bring the bags to the front door. Everyone was waiting on the step as Bernadette's van came down the driveway. "We all wish you a good trip, and thank you for choosing to stay here at the Villa des Violettes," Katherine said as her guests climbed in.

She and Lucille waved from the doorstep.

Kat told Philippe later that she felt like a true *aubergiste*/innkeeper at that moment.

Katherine took care of tasks around the house for the rest of the morning. Play time with six kittens was high on her list. Now five weeks old, they were becoming strong and independent and played constantly when they were not napping. In another three weeks it would be time to send them off to their new homes. Kat and Philippe were thrilled they were not going far away. Simone was going to take one, and Gilles and Christian had chosen the two they wanted. Adorée was going to take one to live with her in Sainte-Mathilde. From the beginning, Kat had felt a strong connection to the runt of the litter and she and Philippe had decided she would stay with them. She had thrived as time went by and was now the troublemaker of the group, always wrestling with her siblings. They decided to call her Bijou after Kat declared one day that she was a gem.

Philippe had a soft spot for the only pure black kitten in the litter. He had started calling him Bonbon, after his favorite black licorice, and it was an easy decision to keep him too.

After a light lunch, Kat took Coco and Rocco for a walk. She went briskly with them on leash along the winding streets over the Cap and down to a small beach where the dogs could play in the sea. On the way back, she kept to the route that she and Philippe had established. It was well away from traffic and the dogs could walk free. Like most well-trained dogs, they chose to stay close to her. All three ended up at Simone's in the afternoon.

The dogs raced to the back garden to visit Victor Hugo and the Twins, and Katherine went inside to the kitchen.

Simone made tea, and Kat told her about what had happened on the motorcycle ride. It upset her to remember it, and Simone gave her a hug and spoke to her soothingly, encouraging her to follow Philippe's advice.

"I understand how difficult it is not to obsess about Delphine. I have been struggling with that too. But our anxiety and concerns will not make anything better. We have to believe that the police are working on this and will find her."

"I understand all that, but my emotions about this are so unpredictable," Kat said. "There are times when I feel almost normal and then suddenly I fall apart. I remember how I felt when I was dealing with my sudden divorce and after my mother died, but this is different because so much is unknown."

"The unknown is what is so difficult to process. Our imaginations take us to very dark places, no question," Simone said.

Katherine described the meeting she had attended with Élise in Nice. "I can't even begin to mention the stories I heard. To think that Delphine might be caught up in anything like that again just makes me crazy. It was bad enough to know from what she told Raymond Albert that she had once been held captive in that sordid world. To think she may have been thrown back into it is almost too much to bear."

"Something unusual occurs when you don't know what has happened," Simone said as she refilled their teacups. "All you know is that the one you love is gone. You don't know if it is forever or not. All of the stages of grief come in and out of your head, jumbled together, and it's impossible to control your emotions. You almost need to tell yourself to walk away, not with your heart, but with your head. You will grieve properly when you truly have something to grieve about."

"Hmmm," Kat mused. "That's more or less what the police who are heading up the investigation in Nice advised as well. Not with words as comforting as yours though!"

"It's easy to say. Not so easy to do, *chérie*," Simone said, and her eyes met Kat's with sympathy and affection. "You are like a daughter to me, and I wish I could ease your pain. I only have words—and a lifetime of experience—to offer. Trust me, I've been where your head is."

Katherine was grateful for Simone's counsel and for her empathy. Fate had brought them together. The ragged hole left in her heart when her mother passed away had been softened and diminished by her friendship with Simone. She knew that Anyu, as Kat called her mother, would be happy that this special woman cared so deeply for her daughter.

"Come," Simone said, "Let's go sit on the terrace. It's a beautiful spring day. Victor and the Twins will be happy to see you."

Kat spent a few minutes giving all the donkeys a good rub on their noses and talking to them as she loved to do. They were such responsive creatures, nuzzling her and grunting their affection. By this time, Rococo were sound asleep in the shade by the side of the villa.

"Would you put up the umbrella, Kat? Then we can sit here at the patio table."

"Did I mention a while ago that André suggested I photograph the Route du Mimosa?" Kat asked as she unfurled the umbrella. "Philippe thinks I should immerse myself in that project for a few days."

"*Bonne idée!*" Simone said. "I would love to go with you."

"Part of it is less than an hour away. So, please do come," Kat said. "Véronique is coming too. What a good time we would have!"

"Ah *chérie*, I know that, and I appreciate your invitation. But you know how much I love being here in my nest. My traveling days are over, even for short trips. But now that you have me texting and messaging on my phone, you can take me along with your photos from there."

"*Bien sûr!* I'll do that with pleasure. We're going to start in Grasse tomorrow and stop by Pégomas before we go to Tanneron and do a hike through part of the mimosa forest. André mentioned that the conditions are just right this year and the show of blossoms is spectacular."

Simone clapped her hands. "In Pégomas you must have *la mimosette*! They only make it at this time of year in the village. It's a brioche decorated with mimosa seeds and filled with a scrumptious flavored cream that is the secret of the *le pâtissier*. *Delicieuse!*"

"We'll bring some back for you because I'll be home by late afternoon. Véronique is going to stay over, and the next day we'll drive the rest of the route to Bormes-les-Mimosas."

"Bormes is so beautiful at this time of year. The color and the fragrance will amaze you!" Simone said. "It truly is the mimosa capital. My memories of it are old but vivid."

Kat grinned. "I've wanted to go there since I read about it years ago. Funny how I dreamed about returning to France for so many years when I was in Toronto and now I live here. I still have to pinch myself some days!"

The two friends sat in the warm sunshine and chatted a while longer.

As she got up to go home, Kat gave Simone a *bise* and held her hand. "Thank you for your wise words. I understand what you were saying to me about Delphine. I will hold her in my heart and get on with life. Hope will never fade."

15

"*W*ait until you see this place," Véronique said, as she and Kat zipped along the auto route toward the exit to Grasse.

Soon they turned up a road that took them into the hills, leaving the coast behind. They talked non-stop all the way. As they drew closer to the town considered the world's capital of perfume, they fantasized about what they might have seen if they had been here centuries ago. There was a time when all the surrounding hillsides were covered in flowers that were handpicked at dawn, when their scent was strongest.

"Just imagine ..." Kat's voice died off as she looked at the passing scenery. "What a fascinating history."

"Most of the flowers required to produce perfume are still grown locally, but some of what is needed is imported," Véronique said. "The perfume companies in Grasse today put on tours that tell you all about the history of the business. If you haven't gone on one, you should."

"Another 'must' to add to my to-do list," Kat said, making a reminder note on her phone. "I should call it my never-ending to-do list. There's always something I don't want to miss!"

"I was astounded the first time I came up to the place I'm taking you to," Veronique said. "When I was working on a tapestry for a show in Cannes a couple of years ago, I heard about this man who was using the original techniques of the 1600s to create wool dye. I wanted a different shade of purple—a pure violet—so I came up here to see what he had."

In the year and a half that they had been friends, Katherine had developed a tremendous respect for Véronique's commitment to her craft of weaving. She was a true artist who used her talent and imagination to create colorful and intricate tapestries and wall hangings.

"So what did you discover?" Kat asked.

"Wait a minute and you will see!"

Moments later, Véronique slowed the car down and took an almost hidden turn off from the main road. They drove down a long laneway, flanked by a thick forest that suddenly changed dramatically. Both women gasped at the explosion of bright yellow blossoms on trees that bordered the lane now. After a short distance, they emerged into a clearing filled with vast flowerbeds green with new growth. The view beyond stretched all the way to the coast.

"*Formidable!*" Véronique exclaimed. "I haven't been here at this time of year before. How spectacular!"

They came to a stop at elaborate wrought-iron gates set in a high fence. Véronique spoke rapidly into an intercom. The gates opened, and they proceeded slowly onto a cobble-stone driveway that led to the far side of the clearing. There an ornate Italian-influenced villa, with bright green glazed roof tiles, glistened in the sun. A central tower dominated the cream-colored marble building. Rows of round-arched windows filled each of the two floors. Ornate doors led out to wide terraces furnished with vintage metal patio tables, lounges and massive planters.

The only time Kat had seen similar architecture was when Philippe surprised her with a quick trip to the Loire valley. Bypassing many jewels of French Renaissance architecture, they had visited a smaller, Italianate chateau similar to this one.

Véronique said, "It's worth the drive just to see this, isn't it?"

Kat's head bobbed with enthusiasm. "This is unbelievable. It is breathtaking. Simply breathtaking. Those mimosas, this view and that villa!"

"It's called the Villa Barolo, and it was built by a famous French perfumer in the early 1800s. He married the daughter of an Italian family whose history went back five centuries. Their descendants still own the property, and various family members spend a good part of the year here."

"Is that who you are meeting today?" Kat asked.

"No, we're meeting the chief gardener and caretaker of the property. His name is Leon, and I have no idea how old he is but he has been on this property for fifty years. He is a magician with plants. They grow particular species here for the local perfumeries. Many years ago, as a hobby, he began to produce dyes from the plants for wool and silk. He makes a purple-violet shade that I used for that Cannes exhibit and have used ever since."

Kat shook her head. "This is another thing that I can't get over, living in France. So often there are unbelievable situations like this—driving onto some amazing property with a story that sounds made up, just to pick up some wool dye."

Véronique laughed. "*Alors!* Not just any old dye, but one

especially made from a plant magician's secret formula. *Oui! C'est la vie en France.*"

Veronique pulled up in front of a cottage at one side of the villa. "I will just be a minute. Would you like to come in with me?"

"Actually, I would love to take a few photos. Do you think anyone would mind?" Kat asked, picking up her camera from the floor where she kept it for quick access.

"It's okay to take pictures of the garden and the view, but not the villa," Véronique said. "I learned that the hard way one of the first times I was here. They protect their privacy at all costs."

"Fair enough," Kat said as she got out of the car and began shooting.

In a few minutes, Véronique emerged from the cottage carrying a small box and accompanied by a man whom she introduced to Kat as Leon. Kat thought he could be a stand-in for Dumbledore and had to stifle a giggle. She accepted his friendly *bises* and enjoyed a few minutes of conversation.

"Madame tells me you are going to Pégomas! I told her you must have at least one *mimosette*! Ha! You will be doing well if you only eat one!" He prattled on in a one-sided conversation about weather, plants and the current political situation.

Véronique took the first chance to interrupt him and said, "We should get on our way, Monsieur Leon. *Mille mercis* for the dye and, as usual, I will send you photos of how I use the wool yarn and silk threads. I don't know any other weaver who has this color, so I feel incredibly blessed."

Leon smiled. "I keep this one just for you, Madame." He took her hand and gently kissed the back of it, before Véronique got back in the car.

As they drove off, Katherine said, "See what I mean? Only here!"

The two friends laughed and chatted as they drove fifteen minutes south to the town of Pégomas. At times the road carved through dense forest and at others through unremarkable commercial and residential areas.

"Here's another thing about living here that I absolutely never get over," Kat said. "I can go out every day and end up in a place I've never seen before. In fact, I may never even have heard of it. Like Pégomas! I've been to Grasse lots of times and to Mougins, for heaven's sake, yet, I've never heard of this town even though it's only a hop, skip and a jump from both of those. It boggles my mind." Her mind shifted gears. "Mougins makes me think about Delphine—there I go again. Since we're so close, maybe we should go by the shelter and see the Alberts."

Véronique replied, "Oh Kat, our little mimosa excursion is supposed to take your mind off Delphine. She is always on my mind too. Let's not go to Mougins. That will only make things worse today, and you are in touch with the Alberts anyway, right?'

Kat nodded. "You're being sensible. Thanks. On to the mimosettes, and if they are that good we can plan to take Delphine there next year. There, that's my positive thought for today."

Véronique smiled and patted Katherine's arm. "*C'est un bon plan!* Let's count on that. Do you know I have never tasted *une mimosette*? There are so many foods particular to one little village or region, it's impossible to eat them all. Which means there's always a new dish or ingredient waiting to be discovered."

"Tell me about it," Kat said. "If I didn't cycle and walk as much as I do, I shudder to think how much I would weigh!"

16

When they arrived in Pégomas, they couldn't find a parking spot. Checking license plates, Véronique said that a lot of the parked cars belonged to tourists. "Are you sure you want to do this?" she asked as she pulled to a halt in front of the boulangerie. There was a long lineup in front of its doors.

"*Totalement!*" Kat assured her. "I wouldn't miss this chance now that we are here. It's part of the adventure."

She got out, and Véronique pulled the car around the corner to wait for her.

"Here you go," Kat said fifteen minutes later, as she handed a mimosette to Véronique and took one for herself from a box of eight more. Another box held a galette. "I had to plead to buy this many, and several people in line with me came to my defense. It was fun. Everyone was so good-natured! I bought the galette for Didier and his crew."

With each bite, they murmured their approval of this new taste sensation.

Véronique said, "*Formidable!* I love the little crystalized mimosa flower on top too. *Mignon!* So sweet!"

Wiping a fleck of mimosa-flavored cream from her cheek, Kat said, "That was worth the drive."

"Speaking of the drive—hold on to your hat, as they say in the States, right? David says it all the time." Véronique said with a twinkle in her eye. "This back road to Tanneron is something else. It's not long, but it's memorable!"

They whooped and laughed as Véronique skillfully navigated the twists and turns of the road that climbed to Tanneron. On the edge of town, they stopped to take in the view across the valleys to Vence, the Baou de Saint-Jeannet, and the Mercantour National Park up in the Alps.

After researching the Tanneron area a few weeks earlier, Kat and Véronique had decided they would pass on the full five-hour hike through the mimosa forest. Photographer friends had given them directions to a spot where they could park and walk through the most impressive part.

"I've got baguette sandwiches and a jug of water in a thermal bag in my backpack, along with my camera lenses and tripod," Kat said, as they put on their hiking shoes.

"Let me put the food in my pack, so you can focus on the work you are here to do. Consider me your assistant today. I've got the GPS in case we get hopelessly lost," Véronique said.

"Thanks! Should we have one more *mimosette* before we set off?"

"Purely for sustenance, of course."

They nibbled on the sweet delicacies as they set off down a well-worn path.

"Everything I've read about this park says this is the largest mimosa forest in Europe," Kat said. "And it all began with one man's idea to bring this plant from Australia to the south of France."

Katherine took several photos with her phone as she

evaluated all the possible shots of the trees surrounding them. Then she got down to more serious work with the camera that had served her so well for many years. She had used some of André's new equipment in the past, but she preferred using her own, experimenting with her new lenses.

After an hour of walking up a gradual incline, sometimes over rugged terrain, and crossings two creeks, they found themselves under a golden canopy of mimosa. The sun filtered through in places, making the bright yellow brilliant. The fragrance was almost overpowering.

Katherine let out a loud sigh. "Now I understand what all the excitement is about. It's a sumptuous fantasy of yellow and gold. What a perfect reminder of the power and beauty of nature. Honestly, I feel like I can hardly breathe."

Véronique nodded. "I've seen mimosas before. But not like this. Our timing could not have been better. *C'est vraiment magnifique!*"

"Truly magnificent! Just ignore me for a while. I'm going to keep taking pictures before other people show up." Kat set up the tripod, carefully taking note of the angle of light and shadows, and adjusting her aperture. It took time to compose and frame the image she hoped for and she lost herself in that diversion. Using a remote trigger for her shutter to keep the camera steady, she took shots from several different perspectives. Her close-ups, taken with the camera's macro settings, captured the fine details of the trees' lacy, fern-like leaves and its tiny sunburst blossoms. Shots she took with her wide-angle lens filled the entire frame with the dense, brilliant yellow forest.

By the time other hikers arrived, Kat and Véronique were ready to move on. After a short walk they came to a clearing that provided stunning views down to the Massif de l'Esterel and the coast. Kat quickly set up her camera again, thankful their timing had worked well.

Véronique found a grassy spot with an unobstructed view and unpacked their picnic. While they ate the tomato and cheese baguette sandwiches, they soaked in their surroundings. They were only half-joking when they talked about stretching out and having a short snooze, but that idea was banished by the arrival of a family with young children and dogs.

"It's definitely time to move on," Véronique said. "Are you satisfied with all you've done, Kat? Would you like to shoot some more?"

Kat shook her head as she packed up her equipment. "This was excellent. I think I've got everything I need for today."

Because they had taken the short trail into the forest, they now had to turn around and retrace their steps to the car. They were both happy to revisit the area with the canopy cover and agreed they had been wise to avoid a possibly grueling uphill climb had they chosen to hike the long trail.

"It feels a bit like cheating," Véronique said as they sat to change their shoes after reaching the car. "But now that I'm seventy-six I feel entitled to take the easy way." They high-fived that comment.

Before leaving, they visited the shops of two *mimosistes*. Both of these farms that specialize in growing mimosas were family run. Their staff gladly spoke about the conditions that made the mimosa forest thrive. Both shops featured displays of their own products, including several different types of honey produced by their apiaries.

The two women took their time returning to Antibes, driving along back roads that wound through many small villages. But, before long, they were back in the thick of busy traffic and commercial development along the coast.

"From one extreme to the other in less than an hour," Kat commented.

"*C'est la vie ici.* And you love it," Véronique replied, and they both laughed.

"Do you think you captured the type of image André is hoping to exhibit in the next gallery show?" Véronique asked.

"We shall see," Kat replied. "As carefully as I plan and set up my shots, I never know for sure my results until I see the photo on my computer screen. Sometimes the shot I took the least time taking is the one that jumps out. As André likes to say, "*On ne sait jamais!*"

Véronique smiled, "True. You just never know."

"I'm so fortunate to have André's support for my photography. The more I work with him, the more I understand how much there is to learn about the craft. One of the reasons Philippe and I are going to Corsica in May is so I can attend a three-day landscape photography workshop André has organized. I can't wait!"

Véronique and David had visited Corsica many times through the years, and Kat plied her with questions on the rest of the way home. She felt relaxed and, for the first time since Delphine's disappearance, she was thinking about something positive in her future.

17

*D*usk was falling as the car neared Antibes, caught now in the usual rush hour congestion. Véronique was just going with the flow, not in any particular hurry.

Katherine answered a call from Philippe. "Where are you, *Minou*? Almost home?"

"Yes, we are about fifteen minutes away. Just moving slowly with the traffic for the moment," she replied.

"Simone called and asked if we would go over to her place right now," Philippe said.

"No problem. We have some mimosettes for her and were going to stop by with them anyway. Is she okay? It's a little strange for her to call at this time of day. Did she say whether she needed something?"

"I'm walking over there now. I asked if anything was wrong, and she told me not to worry, just to come. *Un peu curieux* ..." Philippe's voice faded, and then he exclaimed. "*Mon Dieu!*"

Kat's voice rose, "What? What's the matter?" She could tell from his breathing that he was moving quickly now.

"I just saw Raymond Albert and his wife going into Simone's house. And then I noticed that there's a police car parked behind their van. Bizarre!"

Katherine looked at Véronique, her eyes wide. "Oh my gosh! This must be bad news about Delphine! What else would it be? Oh no!"

Véronique began to drive more aggressively.

"I'm hanging up," Philippe said. "See you shortly."

Katherine began to wring her hands. "*Un peu curieux, bien sûr!* I feel ill! There's only one reason why the Alberts would be there too—and the police."

Véronique glanced over. "*Mais non*, not necessarily. Don't be so quick to jump to that conclusion. Perhaps they are there to give Simone an update on the police investigation."

"Now I think about it, why would they be at Simone's? That doesn't really make a lot of sense." Kat could not think of any reason.

They passed several minutes in silence. Both women were lost in their own thoughts, wondering what they might be facing.

"This does not feel good," Kat said at last.

Véronique agreed, then added, "We have to keep hoping for the best."

"I've been trying to do that for two weeks now. I will never give up. But now I'm terrified by what we might hear." She shuddered involuntarily and rubbed her face. "I've been shaking my head in disbelief for those two weeks too. It seems surreal that this kind of issue has touched our lives. Do you know what I mean?"

Véronique nodded. "We live in a different world these days."

"Let's park at our place and walk over," Kat said as they drove up the street. "Then we won't have to bother with the car after. I'm going to run in and get a shawl. I'm shivering like crazy, but I know it is not from the weather. Would you like something?"

"I'm fine thanks. I'll wait in the front foyer and talk to the dogs—or cats. There are lots of choices at your place these days," Véronique said, hoping to lighten the mood.

Within minutes the two women were walking along the path to Simone's house. Philippe was waiting at the front door. His face showed no emotion as he told Kat he still had no idea what was going on. He said that, when he arrived, Simone had invited him to join the Alberts in the salon. Then she had left the room, saying she would be back shortly.

Kat, Véronique, and Philippe joined Raymond and Marceline Albert in the salon. Simone had placed on the coffee table two olive boards with tapenade, saucissons and freshly sliced baguette, as if they had come for an *apéro*. There were also glasses and a pitcher of water.

Raymond was pacing, and his wife was on the verge of tears. They all exchanged *bises* and confused looks of concern. "*Qu'est-ce qui se passe?*" they whispered. "What is going on?"

Then the door from the kitchen opened, and Simone slowly walked into the room, holding Delphine tightly by the arm.

The young woman's makeup was not as heavy as usual. Some metal studs and eyebrow rings appeared to be missing. But it was their Delphine.

"Our Delphine is home," Simone said in a quiet voice, filled with emotion. Her eyes glistened.

The moment felt unreal to Katherine—a loved one returned from the dead. Stunned silence hung in the air for a moment, and every face betrayed their confused emotions.

Then everyone suddenly burst with joy. Philippe hooted and Véronique cheered. Delphine burst into tears, followed by Kat and Marceline, and rushed into Katherine's arms. Philippe and Raymond sniffled, and Delphine moved from one person to the other, exchanging *bises*. Soon, everyone was entwined in a group hug, arms around each other, with Delphine in the middle of it all. Simone stood to one side with a broad smile that made her glow.

A police officer quietly entered the room.

"*Asseyez-vous tout le monde, s'il vous plaît,*" he politely asked, and they all took a seat.

The cluster of emotion slowly untangled. Kat passed a box of tissues around. Simone disappeared into the kitchen.

The officer remained standing. After introducing himself, he said "I am sure you all have many questions, and I am here to answer them as well as I possibly can, with help from Mademoiselle Delphine."

Simone came back in and sat beside Delphine, taking her hand.

Katherine realized she was holding her breath. Her heart was pounding and her thoughts swirling. *Delphine is alive. She is here, I'm so relieved!*

Delphine said, "I'm so sorry for all the worry and concern I have put you through during the past two weeks. I had no idea what was going to happen when I left the refuge. I thought I would be away for just two days, as I often was."

Raymond and Marceline nodded. "We thought you would be back like always. But then, when you didn't come back, we were afraid to tell anyone," Albert said. "We didn't know what to do. But finally we told Katherine your story, and we all agreed we needed to call the police."

Delphine looked apologetic. "*Désolée.* I put you in a terrible position. I am so sorry. But everything happened so quickly and—"

At this point, the police officer interrupted. He bowed respectfully toward Delphine and said, "Perhaps I should explain and spare you the trauma of reliving the last two weeks."

Delphine smiled weakly and nodded.

"When Delphine went to the safe house as she often did, there was a new young girl there who had escaped from a slavery situation. When she described where she had been held and the man who was her pimp, Delphine was sure she knew this man. The safe-house director contacted us and we showed the girl a file of photos. She pointed to one man, and it was the one Delphine knew."

Delphine raised her hand slightly and looked at the officer. "May I say something?"

He gave her a kindly smile. "*Bien sûr! Comme tu veux!* As you wish, mademoiselle."

Delphine explained, "You will understand this from the story of my past. This was the man—*mon oncle*, they told me, but he wasn't—who kept me at the club from which I escaped." She nodded at the officer.

He continued. "We asked Delphine if she could help us catch him, and she agreed. These are extremely dangerous criminals, and Delphine's safety was of utmost importance to us. Everything had to be completely confidential. She knew you would be worried, but she was more committed to helping us. She had no access to her cell phone and had to completely put her trust in us."

He looked at her with great respect. Then he turned his

gaze back to the others. "This young woman put everything on the line. She wore a disguise and a wire and put herself at risk. There were two undercover agents involved, who did their best to keep Delphine safe at all times. It was not always easy, and she showed tremendous bravery—as well as acting skills. *Mon Dieu!*" He paused for a moment and shook his head.

Delphine blushed. "*Monsieur* ..."

The officer raised his hand to indicate he expected no response from Delphine. His admiration was clear.

He continued. "But we were successful. It was teamwork at its best, and this vile man is now in custody. Some people in his network are as well, more than we hoped. We owe this young woman a tremendous debt of gratitude."

Delphine smiled weakly at the officer, then dropped her gaze as he started to speak again.

"If you have any questions, I can answer some of them. In time, Delphine may share some information with you. But there are many things we cannot answer. Please respect that."

Delphine looked apologetically at Raymond and Marceline. "Thank you for trying to protect me. I'm so sorry I caused you such worry and problems at the refuge by disappearing."

Husband and wife both spoke at once, assuring Delphine that they were simply happy she was safe and well. "All of our volunteers stepped up and helped out. We missed you, but we managed. There will be a grand celebration when you get back."

Katherine spoke up. "Yes, Delphine, we are all so relieved you are safely back. We were all so worried and ... terrified ... and ... Was that you in the blonde wig last weekend in Pont du Loup? Was I right?"

Delphine looked at the police officer who nodded slightly.

"Yes, Katherine. It was. I was made up to look like I did when that man was my pimp. And it worked. He thought he was going to get me back into his business."

"I was right, after all! I just knew it!" Katherine exclaimed. Philippe put his arm around her and said, "*Tout à fait!* You were absolutely sure."

The officer told them that they had made their arrests on Sunday. "Since then, Mademoiselle Delphine has stayed with the staff at the safe house. She has continued to help with the new arrivals and has also talked with social workers and counsellors herself. It was of concern to us that she receive the help she required."

Delphine assured everyone that she felt fine now. "Having this whole situation play out the way it did gave me some closure for what I went through years ago. Talking with counsellors these last few days was immensely helpful too."

The police officer asked if everyone was satisfied he had answered their questions. Then he reminded them of the confidential nature of what had taken place and repeated that they not discuss it with anyone else. They all agreed.

After the officer left, Simone asked Philippe to bring in champagne from the kitchen. "I prepared the glasses and tray for you. This is certainly a moment to celebrate."

A toast was made to Delphine and there were more tears, this time of relief and happiness.

Delphine looked around at everyone. "At night, as I tried to fall asleep, I would think about how fortunate I am to have you all in my life. You have become my family, and that helped give me the strength to go through with this scheme. I've learned so much from all of you about the love and trust a family shares. Sometimes I was frightened, but even more so I was determined to get this man off the street. It is so satisfying to know we did it."

"Are you coming back to the refuge now?" Raymond asked.

"If it is fine with you," Delphine answered. "I would like to stay here with Simone and Katherine and Philippe for a day or two. Then I will be back with you and all of our four-legged friends. I bet there are a few new ones."

Simone sent a text to Didier so they would know Delphine was safely back and with her, and then gently hinted that she and Delphine felt exhausted and needed to sleep.

Véronique, Katherine and Philippe strolled back to the villa in moonlight that washed over the few mimosas that were in bloom along the way. The women described their day in the forest to Philippe.

"I didn't realize we had any mimosas until they burst into flower last month," Kat said. "I'm sure the garden has many other surprises for us too. Auguste has cleared away so much overgrowth and opened up areas we thought were hopeless."

"Kat calls him the gentle giant and the name is most appropriate," Philippe added.

"He is now trying to bring the potager here back to life, and he's making great progress," Kat told Véronique. "I'm excited about having a kitchen garden for the first time!"

When they got to the house, Katherine looked at her watch and said to Véronique. "All right, in one hour it will be time for my weekly video chat with Molly. She will be delighted to see you and happy to hear the good news about Delphine. She's been sending messages the whole time telling me that she and Tony were praying for her."

"Excellent!" Véronique said. "It will be great to chat with Molly. In the meantime, I must call David and let him know what has happened. He will be overjoyed to know Delphine is safe."

Philippe and Kat went out to the garden with Rococo, throwing sticks and giving them a good play time before bed. Belle kept them company while prowling for a nocturnal creature for her to pounce on. When the dogs were too tired to run anymore, they all went inside to the salon to wait until it was time to chat with Molly. Kat brought in the box which Belle and the kittens had made their home again for the moment.

At the appointed time, Kat's phone rang with Molly's video call. She answered on her tablet and set it on the coffee table so they could all see each other.

Véronique laughed at Molly's usual lively greeting.

"*Bonsoir* Katski! And how is *la vie en rose* in beautiful Cap d'Antibes tonight?"

"You aren't going to believe what we have to tell you today!" Kat replied.

18

*S*hortly after sunrise Didier, Auguste, Alfonso, and Alejandro arrived at Simone's door, each carrying a bouquet of flowers.

"Delphine is still asleep, but she will be touched by your thoughtfulness," Simone told them. "*Entrez, mes garçons.* Let me make you a coffee or tea and answer some of your questions."

She took a sheet of madeleines from the oven and set them on a rack on the counter to cool.

"*C'est un miracle de Dieu!*" Didier said, and all four men crossed themselves and looked to the ceiling.

"Yes. A true miracle from God," Alfonso whispered, his voice full of emotion.

Simone answered their questions as best she could as they sipped their espressos and ate a madeleine or two. She promised to let them know when Delphine was awake and ready for company. "She will want to see you. *Absolument.*"

As the men were leaving to set about their work for the day, Alfonso hung slightly behind.

"*S'il vous plaît, Madame, donnez-lui ces papiers. C'est ma poésie.*" He said shyly as he handed Simone a thick bundle of papers, his poetry, clipped together.

Simone assured him, with a warm smile, that she would be certain to give them to Delphine as soon as she woke up.

As Alfonso followed the others over to the Villa des Violettes, Simone felt a rush of affection for him. His feelings for Delphine were obvious.

The madeleines waiting in the kitchen for Delphine were still warm when she finally surfaced. "That was the best sleep I have had for two weeks," she said. "As you might imagine."

"*Mon ange*, you must rest as much as you feel necessary. The more I learn about your trials of the past two weeks, the more I want to be sure you are taking care of yourself now. We are all here to help you do this."

Delphine began to answer but suddenly brought her hands to her mouth as she was consumed by a long drawn-out yawn. "*Pardon!*" she apologized. "*Tu as raison.* You are right. I'm feeling quite exhausted."

Simone pointed to the flowers, which she had arranged in vases. "Didier and his crew each brought you a bouquet."

"How sweet of them," Delphine replied. "I will go over and see them later and drop by Kat's place."

"And Alfonso has left you this," Simone said with a smile, pointing to the clipped bundle on the counter.

Delphine blushed and blinked rapidly.

"All four of *les garçons* worked hard distributing flyers about your disappearance. They never stopped trying to turn up some clue as to what had happened to you. Everyone refused to give up."

Delphine sniffled and reached for a tissue. "How kind. I am just realizing what a problem I caused. I'm so touched by all the efforts everyone made. I had no idea."

Simone patted her hand. "What you did was brave and selfless. Who could have imagined this would occur and play out the way it did? The police had no choice but to keep everything completely confidential, although they did hint to Philippe that they had a handle on what was happening. And a few of my contacts sent me cryptic messages, which I took to mean that you were in their care. But of course neither of us really knew what had happened to you."

"I'm so sorry that I could not let you, or anyone else, know what I was doing," Delphine said.

Simone threw her hands in the air. "The human trafficking! Girls forced into the sex trade—in our own towns. Of course, we were aware. *Désolée*, as so often happens, it is only when a situation touches close to home that we take action. Now we must try to be involved in other ways. Who knows how many young girls are being helped by this police operation."

Delphine nodded. "We can only hope. *Hônnetement*, coming so close to that awful world again made me even more aware of what a threat it is. The girls that get involved are all vulnerable and in need of protection, and they believe the promises they are given. What's worse now is the major role that drugs play in controlling their lives. Many of the girls are addicts. The traffickers keep them supplied, but only if they cooperate. I was so scared and sickened by what I saw. Simone, we need to keep fighting this. I hope you can advise me on what to do because I don't want to stop now."

Simone's voice was low but strong when she answered. "In my long life I have seen how every generation has its own evils to fight. But my heart breaks for what I see happening today. I wish I could have fifty years back to be strong and join your fight. But I will do whatever I can, in my own way, and I will support your efforts one hundred percent. Katherine made some good contacts in Nice, and perhaps you can begin there. I know she and Véronique want to help."

Delphine smiled and stood up. "There's much to think about. Now I'm going to have a shower and start the day. Thank you, dear Simone, for everything."

"This is your home, *mon ange*," Simone replied. "Your room is always ready for when you want to stay. Wait until you see how the kittens have grown next door. Did you know I am taking one of them?"

Simone's cell phone rang. Katherine was calling to invite Delphine and Simone over for lunch. Simone declined, "*Merci, mais je suis fatiguée!* The drama and emotion of last night have drained me of energy. I am going to rest but will send Delphine to you."

Delphine nodded. "Please tell her I am going to stop by the stable first. I'll be there in an hour."

Katherine saw Delphine walking along the driveway from the stable and opened the doors for the dogs to go out. They immediately raced over to her and she knelt to hug them while they squirmed and bounced around her. Kat followed them and, once the joyful reunion calmed down, she wrapped her arms around Delphine. They stood in the driveway, enveloped in each other's arms for a long minute.

"I still can't believe you are here. But you are really back! I was so frightened we would never see you again," Kat said.

"I don't know when I've ever been so scared. But you must have been even more terrified."

"*En fait, non*," Delphine replied. "Strange as it may sound, I wasn't terrified. Sometimes I was scared that we were not going to catch Armand, my persecutor, and the main guy we were after. And that would have been awful. But I really did not fear for my safety because an undercover officer was always with me. I didn't have time to think about the risks. We were working all the time, building a web we could lure Armand into."

"I can't imagine—" Kat murmured.

"I don't know if I can explain it fully, but I was driven by anger and hatred for all he did to me in the past. Everything I had bottled up rose to the surface, and I just knew I wanted to do everything I could to get even and to stop him from inflicting the same hell on other young women."

"It's impossible to grasp how you, our sweet quiet Delphine, turned into Wonder Woman!" Kat blurted.

Delphine slipped her arm through Kat's as they walked back to the villa, trailed by Rococo. "I'm a bit shocked myself, but the empowerment I felt when the police took Armand away is something I will never forget. *Ce monstre!* That monster is pure evil!"

As they walked into the house, Kat said, "Lunch is ready, whenever you are."

"What I'm ready for is to play with the pups and cuddle those kittens of yours," Delphine sighed. "Isn't it wonderful that Simone is taking one? I want to get back to the real world and spend time with what pleases me most—four-footed creatures."

"Now that sounds like the sweet Delphine we know and love," Kat said and gave Delphine a grin.

"*Je suis de retour*. I am back!" Delphine declared.

19

*T*he following weeks at the Villa des Violettes were filled with activity.

The potager was slowly being filled with herbs and flowers as the planting season settled in. Kat appreciated the time Auguste spent on the project. Planning the beds was one thing, he told her, but planting them was another. "It must all please your heart," he said. "The potager is like a canvas and you make it your work of art."

This advice reminded her of how much she had to learn about gardening. She did know that it felt satisfying to dig her hands into the soil and she recalled the peace her mother had found working in her gardens. Kat was happy to have not just Auguste to help with the potager but also to have her cousin Andrea offer advice from their organic farm.

Some sections were planted according to the compatibility of color, texture and size. Annuals were mixed with perennials, and vegetables with flowers. After careful research, Kat decided to include sunflowers, nasturtiums and marigolds, which would grow from seeds sown in the ground.

Auguste added, "*Et bourrache*—borage—*c'est necessaire.*" He described the star-shaped blue flowers and said how they attracted bees. He knew that Kat was especially keen to tempt butterflies and bees into the garden.

Luxurious mounds of lavender had bordered the original potager and these were replanted in long rows at the front and the back of the new garden plan. Auguste explained that this would allow the fragrance and the bees to be in all corners during the blooming season.

Kat and Philippe had agreed to his suggestion that they build a few apiaries at the back of the garden.

Belle padded softly through each section of the potager, carefully stepping between the new plants as she asserted her proprietary rights. *It's as if she knows the dogs will not be allowed in here*, Kat thought as she watched her.

She could hardly contain her excitement while the chicken coop and fenced run were being constructed and made ready for occupancy. Adorée and her friend, Maxim, were going to deliver hens, young chicks and a fine rooster —Adorée's words—as soon as they got the go ahead when Kat and Philippe returned from Corsica.

In practice for that holiday, Kat and Philippe went out on the Ducati a few times a week.

"We've got to work on our riding muscles," Philippe told her after she mentioned she was getting a few aches and pains after each short trip. "These are different from our cycling muscles."

Most recently they had ridden west through the red hills of the Massif de l'Esterel.

"This is nothing," Philippe told her when she exclaimed at the beauty, "Wait until you see Corsica!"

Kat talked excitedly about the trip in her weekly video chat with Molly.

"We will be off to Corsica before we know it," Kat exclaimed.

"Tell me the details " Molly said, " so I can go with you to Corsica vicariously."

"Philippe is planning most of it. All I know is that we will take Jean-Luc's ashes with us and try to find Simone's former hideaway there. I'm going to do a three-day land-scape photography workshop that André is leading for six of us. Otherwise, our itinerary is pretty wide open and we will play it by ear—at least that's all I can get out of Philippe at the moment."

"Sounds awesome!" Molly exclaimed. "Send tons of photos."

"You can bet on that," Kat said.

"Remember to take extra cushioning for your butt!" Molly added.

"That too!" Kat agreed, laughing at such a classic Molly comment.

"How are the kittens doing?" Molly asked. "Let's see them please!"

Kat quickly went to find them. She returned with two fluffy bundles, one gray and one black as coal, still small enough to hold by one arm.

"They are so cute," Molly squealed. "Have you chosen names yet? It must seem strange to have only two of them in the house now."

"Finally!" Kat laughed. "Bijou is the silvery grey female and Bonbon is the black as licorice male."

Molly fussed over them both. "Those are perfect names."

"And you are right, we do miss having all six of them. It

was such fun, but we knew it had to end. Simone and Adorée adore their kittens, and Gilles and Christian are crazy about theirs. So it's all good! And they are still in the family so we get to see them all the time."

"And those rambunctious pups? How do they feel about feline interlopers into their kingdom?"

"We often find all four curled up together. It's so cute! I think they've taken over the mothering from Belle who is happy to be back outside chasing mice."

"Will Delphine stay at the villa while you are away?" Molly asked.

"Yes, thank goodness it's not a long drive and her hours are flexible. She'll go back and forth to the shelter each day. She has settled back into her regular routine, with one exception. Now she spends every weekend at Simone's. Did I tell you I saw some of Delphine's artwork when Monsieur Albert showed me her room. It was amazing!"

"I vaguely remember you saying that, but I didn't pay much attention since we were busy worrying about her," Molly said.

"Well, she had been painting all the time at the refuge and told me it was Simone's artwork that inspired her. Now they paint together on weekends, and it is so good for both of them. Simone says she is most content to be alone, but I can see how she is enjoying the company. Delphine is a great help to her, without being intrusive. Even Victor Hugo and the Twins seem more full of life with her being around Simone's house as often as she is."

Molly suddenly became animated. "That is great news. And ... hey! ... Thank you for those photos of the violets in bloom! It's one of my favorite memories from last year when I was there with you."

Kat grinned. "I know! It was such a thrill to step outside last week and see the purple explosion again!"

She had sent photos to Molly of the wild violets that gave the Villa des Violettes its name. Early in March, the tiny plants burst into blankets of purple haze, and the effect was breathtaking. Her first sighting of the violet flowers carpeting their entire property had stopped Katherine in her tracks, as it had the previous year. A deep purple hue spread over the grass and through the gardens and wooded areas, running like a river to the stone wall that overlooked the sea. A sweet perfume lightly filled the air.

"And we didn't have any guests that week," Kat lamented. "If only the flowers lasted longer."

"The violets are your harbingers of spring, Katski. It's still frickin' freezing here! We could use some of what you have. I'm so happy everything sounds good again. Give Delphine a *bise* from me and let her know we were praying for her every day."

On the last Sunday in March, Philippe handed the care of his market stall to Gilles and Christian for a few days. He and Kat loaded the car with dogs, flowers, and cheese and set off for Sainte-Mathilde. They were anxious about Oncle François's health. Joy had let them know that he had been ill and had attended a number of appointments with doctors and physiotherapists. They were under strict instructions from Joy to be there in time for the Sunday family lunch.

"I still haven't quite adjusted to not taking wine when we go somewhere for a meal. It's what we all do in Canada," Kat said. "It feels odd not to."

Philippe chuckled, "And especially when one is visiting a vineyard."

"I'm glad we decided to drive rather than go on the Ducati," Kat said. "It's still a bit nippy for that."

"We would have had a problem bringing all of this stuff with us, particularly those two." He gestured over his shoulder to Coco and Rocco, who were comfortably settled in the back seat, eyes bright with anticipation.

Kat reached back and gave each of them a scratch on the head. "They have one hundred percent enthusiasm for whatever is happening. They make everything an adventure."

They made good time. In spite of the perfect blue-sky day for a drive, there was a noticeable lack of traffic. They sang along to Zaz and chatted about all that was going on in their lives.

Delphine's story was still keeping their heads spinning. After her return, she and Kat had attended a meeting in Nice with the group of women Élise had introduced Kat to. Afterward, Kat told Philippe that she could see the impact of Delphine's words on the group. "I've agreed to go with her wherever and whenever she is asked to speak. She will be a driving force in mobilizing people to help stop human trafficking along the coast."

"She's showing such strength in turning the nightmare of her past into something that will help others."

"I'm so proud of her! You know, I think the fact that she now spends her weekends at Simone's house has influenced her in important ways. An added bonus is the advice Simone is giving her about painting. Simone is so happy to be a mentor to her."

"And Alfonso is so happy to have her as his muse for his *poesie. Il y a de la passion!*" Philippe said with a grin.

Kat laughed with him. "Romance is in the air, for sure! It's sweet to watch those two dancing around each other. They are both so shy, and Delphine will need time to learn to trust her heart."

After an hour, they turned off the auto route on to the first of the back roads that Philippe knew so well and that would take them to Sainte-Mathilde. Now, vineyards, orchards and pastures filled Kat's field of vision.

"Sunday is a good day to drive up here," she said, "As much as I love the coast, I always feel a growing sense of peace as we get farther into the countryside. Look at the beautiful white haze over those orchards. Are those almond trees in bloom?"

Philippe nodded. "*Tu as raison.* You are right. Even though spring is officially here, everything is only now waking up. After the cold winter we've had, some plants might be a bit delayed. But the blossoms never disappoint. Gardeners usually wait to plant outside until Saints de Glace day, which is always around May 11."

"The Saints de what day?" Kat asked. "Another one I don't know about?"

"The Ice Saints day—Saint Mamert, Saint Servais and Saint Pancrace. We have a saying, '*Avant Saint Servais, point d'été, après Saint Servais, plus de gelée.*' You translate please."

Kat thought for a moment then ventured, "Before Saint Servais—I guess they mean the feast of Saint Servais—there's no summer, after the feast of Saint Servais, more jelly? What the ...?"

Philippe chuckled. "Good try. '*Plus de gelée*' is a phrase that means it is safe to plant—no frost. It had to rhyme!"

Kat laughed. "As usual, it sounds better in French. In Canada, we wait until after May 24."

Before long, they turned onto the driveway to Joy's

manor house. In the garden along the driveway bright yellow forsythia was in magnificent bloom, and in front of the manor house, two stunning magnolia trees were already beginning to drop their petals on the path to the front door.

"*Le printemps est arrivé ici!*" Philippe announced. "Spring is definitely here," Kat echoed. "How beautiful!"

The official greeter came bounding out to see them.

"Pico! You sweet boy! We're so happy to see you!" Kat and Philippe said as Picasso, the big yellow Lab, went from one to the other, his tail wagging furiously. As soon as Philippe let Rococo out of the car, the three dogs were off and running.

Joy and her son Henri had followed Picasso from the house and they all exchanged warm *bises*. "*Bienvenue!* You somehow managed to plan a date almost all of us could make, two grandchildren excepted," Joy said. "It's not quite warm enough for *al fresco* dining today so we will be in the dining room. Let me help you with some of your things."

Adorée came running out. "Papa! MamaKat! I'm so happy to see you!" Adorée's years working in London had made her comfortable with hugging, and now she gave each of them what she called a 'squeezy' hug.

They went into the kitchen first to say hello to Antoine and Hélène, the elderly couple who helped run the manor, and to leave the cheese and flowers. Katherine knew from past visits that the flowers would soon reappear on the dining table in Joy's glass vases from Biot. Hélène would make a fuss about the fact they were from Kat and Philippe. It was part of the tradition. The cheese would be presented with another grand flourish at the end of the meal.

Kat knew that this couple was an integral part of the family, and had been for fifty years. Yet they would never consider sitting down to eat with the family. They were happy to stay in their service roles, which were valued and respected. They, and everyone else, understood they were the ones who made these family gatherings so enjoyable, thanks to their cooking and organization. It was a different way of life that Kat had gradually come to appreciate.

The rest of the family was in the salon, with cherished Oncle François the center of attention. He was seated in his favorite armchair by the fireplace and a smile lit his face as Kat and Philippe went straight to him. Champagne was chilling on the sideboard, and two glasses were waiting for Kat and Philippe. A flurry of greetings ensued and then toasts were made to the successful gathering of almost all the family.

"*C'est déjà un miracle!*" Joy said as she raised her glass. Then she raised her glass again and they toasted Delphine's safe return. Philippe had told Joy about her disappearance, and the family had put up flyers in the Luberon area to help. Kat and Philippe filled them in now on Delphine's reappearance and answered their many questions.

Soon they were all seated around the dining room table, and the meal began with two entrées: *escargots à la Bourguignonne*, accompanied by a fresh crusty baguette to sop up the garlicky butter sauce, and *petits farcis*, small vegetables stuffed with a sausage and breadcrumb mix, which had become Kat's favorites.

A lime sorbet, *un trou normand*, cleansed their palates before the main courses, *les plats principaux*.

Joy seldom served only one choice. Today there were two: a delicately seasoned white fish and her legendary *coq au vin*.

"You know I only like to serve *coq au vin* in the cold months. I thought today might be my last opportunity," Joy said, as the dish was passed around the table to murmurs of delight .

Rice, boiled potatoes with parsley, and vegetables steamed until they were tender but still *al dente* rounded out the course. Then a salad of mixed greens with a vinaigrette dressing preceded a cheese platter that drew applause and cheers of "*Bravo Philippe!*"

Always happy to talk about his favorite topic, he explained the choices he had made for today's meal after consulting Joy about the menu.

"First we have Tante Joy's favorite Comté. Next, an Ossau-Iraty made by shepherds in the Pays Basque. I received a delivery this week, so your tastebuds are in for a treat. For Oncle François, but I know he will share, a creamy chèvre from the mountain goat farm of our friend, Jacques, near Entrevaux. And, *comme d'habitude*, as usual, a delicious Brie accompanied by a selection of Hélène's tastiest *confitures*."

Katherine smiled as she considered how Philippe had made cheese such a special part of her new life. Who would have ever imagined?

Dessert was Hélène's famous chocolate mousse, prepared with a recipe she had not divulged through the fifty years of making it. A selection of *petits gourmands*, miniature sweet desserts, accompanied this.

"*C'était délicieux, ma tante,*" Kat told Joy.

Oncle François made a short speech about the joys of sharing a family meal, which made some of them reach for a tissue. Then he made them all laugh when he recited a line about the skin on his tummy being too tight from a familiar French ditty: "*J'ai la peau du ventre bien tendue.*" Everyone burst into that old familiar song and left the table in good humor.

As the others were preparing to leave, Joy took Kat and Philippe aside. "You must go to Adorée's now and see what she has accomplished. She is becoming *une vraie fermière*," she said

"A real farmer! What a lovely compliment! We can't wait to see," Kat said. She had already let Joy know that they would spend the rest of the day with their daughter and return to the manor in the evening. Oncle François was also spending the night at Joy's, so they would have more time together.

20

*K*atherine and Philippe were both grinning as they drove up to the house Adorée had lived in since suddenly leaving her job in London the previous autumn. The property was within easy walking distance of Joy's, but they drove because they had gifts in the car for their daughter.

"The little yellow house with the blue shutters," Kat said. "Remember Adorée telling us that this is how the cottage has been known in the village since forever? It's the kind of provençal house that makes my heart sing."

Philippe smiled. "I still cannot believe that Adorée has adjusted to this life. I thought she would just stay to help Marie-Claire for a week or two until they found someone permanent. *Mais non!* Here she remains, and she is loving it."

For two years, Adorée had lead the exciting life of an up and coming twenty-something in London, including a high-paying job in investment banking, great friends, and a handsome fiancée. Then she learned on Facebook that he was also a cheating fiancée. That life came to an abrupt end, and she fled to the arms of her beloved Tante Joy, not wanting to bring her crisis into Kat and Philippe's new life together. Of course, when they later discovered this, they scolded her for not coming to them. It had all worked out for the best because she soon and unexpectedly found herself leading a new life in every respect.

An eighty-two-year-old friend of Joy's, Marie-Claire Bellefleur, was being hospitalized indefinitely. She desperately hoped to find someone to take care of her home, which had been in her family for five generations. The property included an enormous potager and an assortment of chickens, which provided multi-colored eggs which she sold at a weekly market stall.

Joy had encouraged Adorée to help Mme. Bellefleur out by looking after the cottage and the flock of chickens for a few days. Six months later, Adorée was still there and had embraced the life completely. It was apparent Marie-Claire would never be able to return from the long-term-care facility. She and Adorée had become close friends, and Adorée remained committed to helping her. She had fallen in love with the life. And possibly also her neighbor Maxim.

Her parents' concerns about how she would support herself were soon allayed. Adorée set up a small online finance-related consulting business, which paid most of the bills. She worked at it one full day a week and most evenings after her chores were completed. She often commented that she had fallen into a rhythm and balance in her life that gave her great satisfaction.

"I loved the fast life in the city while I had it," she told Kat one day, "and now I don't miss it at all. No one is more surprised than I am, but there you go!"

Adorée greeted them now on the path to the front door and took some of the boxes they were carrying.

"*Merci mille fois* for these goodies. Always appreciated. Where are the dogs? I expected them too."

Philippe shook his head. "We decided your flock of chickens would be too much temptation for Rococo. It would be a new experience for them and the chase would be on. We opted for a calm visit with you."

Katherine remembered, from their visit before Christmas, how appealing this simple home was. It was sparsely but comfortably furnished. The ceilings were low with broad oak beams. There were cracks in some of the walls and the whitewash had become patchy. Adorée told them she thought it just added to the character of the place, which made Kat smile at her youthful sense of adventure. A couch and two plump-cushioned chairs upholstered in a faded blue provençal pattern were clustered around the hearth. A battered cast-iron stewing pot hung from a hook centered over the deep, blackened fireplace.

"I can understand completely why you love living here," Kat said. "It's so cozy. I keep thinking about that beautiful bedroom you have upstairs, with all those chockful bookshelves."

Adorée nodded. "Marie-Claire said I could freshen the walls upstairs with new paint. Want to see?" She gestured to the narrow, steep stairs that led up to the bright, spacious bedroom with its own little terrace.

"Yes, I do," Kat said. "But let's go out back first. How is your potager doing? And the chickens? I'm dying to see."

"I was hoping you would say that!" Adorée's eyes were shining. "I'm so excited about you and Papa getting your own potager going at the villa this spring."

Philippe's gaze shifted from one woman to the other, both of whom he loved fiercely, enjoying the close relationship they shared.

Adorée took them through the kitchen to the French doors leading outside.

"*Bienvenue* to my little corner of paradise!" She said, gesturing at the vast vegetable and flower beds and the fruit trees at the rear. In some places, dried vines climbed on otherwise empty frames. What straw mulch had not been blown away by the mistrals lay on the soil in patches. In the beds, vivid green shoots were announcing the arrival of spring, and it was obvious most of the soil had been turned over, ready for planting.

Philippe clapped his hands in appreciation of her efforts and congratulated Adorée with an enthusiastic "*Chapeau!*"

"Yes, hat's off to you!" Kat said. "You've been busy back here." Then she jumped and let out a shriek. A blur of iridescent blackish-green feathers hurtled at her, emitting an ungodly noise.

"Don't worry, MamaKat, that's just Luigi. Remember? The king of the potager," Adorée explained, as she grabbed the rooster. "He is all swagger and no threat. That's the way he reacts to any stranger coming into his territory. *Il est vraiment un gros nounours* … he's really a big teddy bear!"

Holding him in her arms, Adorée stroked Luigi's feathers and cooed softly to him. He pecked gently at her nose and eyed Kat and Philippe suspiciously.

"*Eh bien, bonjour Luigi!*" Kat said, reaching out to stroke him as well. "I do remember you. In fact, I think we went through this on our previous visit. How could I forget? *Pardonnez-moi!*"

By this time, a large flock of chickens of assorted colors and sizes had gathered around them.

"Oh, I love this! They're so friendly and funny." Kat laughed as the chickens inspected her shoes. "I can't wait until we get everything ready for our chickens. I have much to learn from you about keeping them, dear girl."

The late hours of the afternoon passed quickly. They agreed they could not eat another big meal until the next day, after Joy's lavish *dejeuner*, so Adorée prepared *petits goûts* and poured them each an *apéro,* and they chatted into the early evening.

Adorée was curious about what had happened to Delphine and expressed her relief that she was safely back. "I'm so impressed at her commitment to work with others who have been affected by human trafficking. Especially after all she herself went thought. It's so scary … and so out there these days."

Katherine told her about the education program Delphine described they were working on to take into the school system for teenagers.

"We all have heard of horrendous situations because of connections made on social media," Adorée said. "It's the curse of today's world in some ways, yet it's a big part of the culture of people my age and younger. You know I am on Facebook, Instagram, Messenger … and others … with my friends all the time. We do practically everything on our phones."

Kat replied, "And there's no question there are a lot of good things about social media. One has to use it wisely."

Adorée nodded. "Anything else is asking for trouble. I'm going to contact Delphine and see how I can get involved in this in our community. She is truly inspiring me."

Kat and Philippe agreed this would be a fine idea. "The more it is talked about and brought out in the open, the better it is for everyone," Kat said.

When Philippe casually asked about Adorée's handsome

and helpful neighbor, Max, she dodged his question and changed the subject with a shy smile.

"Why don't you bring Tante Joy and Oncle François here for *le petit dejeuner* tomorrow morning? *À dix heure*? That would make me very happy," she said

"*Bonne idée!* Ten o'clock sounds fine. I will ask them as soon as we get back to the *manoir* and let you know. I'm sure they will be delighted!" Kat replied.

A small fire was burning in the fireplace of Joy's cozy parlor when Katherine and Philippe returned. The pleasing scent of dried *garrigue* burning with the wood filled the air with hints of lavender, thyme, and rosemary.

"We lit the fire, not because we need it, but because we love it," Joy explained, as Oncle François nodded. "It will soon be too warm to light a fire indoors."

"The smell always reminds me of my youth." François sounded melancholic. "I seem to be spending a lot of time these days in remembering the past. It is so much better to recall those happy times and let go of the bad."

His comment prompted the four of them to share memories of their childhoods, some of them so funny they filled the room with laughter. But after a while Oncle François grew philosophical. "As the years advance, and I am able to do less, to get around less, I find myself wondering if there is any point to a life like this. Getting old has suddenly become difficult, which I never imagined."

"Mon oncle," Katherine said, taking his hand and looking deeply into his eyes, "Delphine told us she has learned so much from you and Simone about moving forward with her life. You still have much to give all of us. I will never forget how your words influenced me that first time I was in Paris. If it had not been for that conversation with you, I would not be sitting here today. I would not be Madame Dufours. How can I ever thank you for that?"

"More importantly, how can I ever thank you for that?" Philippe added, putting his arm around Kat's shoulders.

It was just the right moment for humor.

Joy rose from her chair and went to her brother-in-law's side. "*Mon cher François*, we have lived so much of life together, for over fifty years, since I married your dear departed brother. We have memories that only we can share. How could I get along without your friendship and your company? You must promise never to abandon me."

She gave him a *bise* on each cheek and then picked up the most recent *Guide Michelin* from a side table. Holding the iconic red-covered book, which lists the top dining places in France, in front of Oncle François, she placed his hand on it. "Please swear on this French bible that you will always be by my side to laugh and to cry together."

François smiled as he placed his hand on the famous book. "*Je te le jure, ma belle-soeur*. I swear. How can I refuse a promise on our *Guide rouge*? I will encourage this weary body to keep going."

On that lighter note, they wished each other good night.

"We can sleep in if we so desire," Joy said, "or we can go for an early morning walk before we go to Adorée's. I have let Antoine and Hélène know we will be away for breakfast."

Philippe and Katherine put on their coats and went out to call Rococo, who had been outside with Picasso for hours. As Kat stood waiting with Philippe on the terrace, she looked up at the glittering star-filled sky. "It's such a beautiful evening. There always seem to be so many more stars in the sky up here in the Luberon. I'm so glad we came and had this family time together."

Philippe drew her close and kissed her forehead. "Yes, the night sky here always appears more intense and dramatic to me. I'm glad we are here too. I think our conversation tonight with Oncle François was important for him. We all need to be reminded of how valued we are to each other, but especially when age is creeping up."

"I could really feel that too. And wasn't Joy hilarious, having him swear on the *Guide Michelin*?"

"*Que demander de plus?*" Philippe said. "In France, what could be better?"

The dogs were bouncing around them now, eager for their bedtime treats, which they wolfed down before bounding up the stairs and following Kat and Philippe into their bedroom. In minutes they all were ready for bed.

"Those pups will sleep well tonight, *mon chou*," Kat said.

"*Bien sûr!*" Philippe replied, as he turned down the duvet. "And we will sleep well too, although there are a few memories I would like to recall with you once you come to bed."

Kat felt a warm rush of emotion deep in her core. "*Avec plaisir, mon amour*," she whispered, and she slipped into his waiting embrace.

21

"*A*pril came in like a lamb," Katherine commented to Philippe one morning. He looked at her in confusion. When she explained the aphorism she was putting a twist on, she discovered this was not a saying in France.

Life had settled down over the last few days, with no new dramas or crises.

Delphine was busy at the shelter. They were always inundated with new arrivals in the spring. She had come to terms remarkably well with the whole episode of working with the undercover police. She had agreed, without hesitation, to return to the safe house from time to time to help counsel frightened new arrivals. She had also committed to volunteering each month with the women's organization for missing girls in Nice.

Kat could sense a new empowerment within Delphine. She initiated conversations more often, and her focus was not always on caring for animals, as it had been. Simone also noticed that Delphine was opening herself to more of life and mentioned this to Kat.

It was obvious to Kat that Delphine's weekends with

Simone were giving both of them a lift. When she commented on this to Philippe, he responded by quoting Victor Hugo. "Life's greatest happiness is to be convinced we are loved." They agreed that Delphine was now beginning to realize how loved she was by the people closest to her.

"And Alfonso's attentions are not going unnoticed," Kat added. "Delphine's face turns a brilliant pink whenever we mention his name. Something is definitely happening there and it's so sweet."

Didier and his team were making headway on the restoration of the stable, although there still was a long way to go. Their attention to detail in using traditional materials and construction methods, all carefully overseen by one of the town's building inspectors, meant progress was slow. On top of this, acquiring the special permits they needed, each of which prompted an inspection, slowed work down to a snail's pace.

"*C'est la France*," everyone said, with a classic Gallic shrug. While they waited for permits and inspections, all of Didier's men worked on reducing the long list of other construction projects on the property.

The gardens were filled with shrubs in flower and blossoms on the fruit trees, and new shoots and buds were appearing daily in the flower beds. Kat was delighted every time she inspected the latest growth.

The carpet of violets was beginning to fade. Kat had captured it in photos at its peak and now as the weather warmed up, the blooms were becoming fewer.

The potager was waiting until after the Saints de Glace for the introduction of delicate annual plants. In the meantime, Philippe and August were digging in peat moss and seaweed fertilizer. "This is a never ending project, *n'est-ce pas*? We will have to do this every year, " Philippe said to Auguste, who nodded in return.

Working by the front doors, planting the pots on either side, Kat was thinking what a warm welcome all the flowers would give to their guests. She buried her nose in the stunning cascade of mauve and purple blossoms on the wisteria vine that wrapped around the doors. They had begun to bloom just days earlier, and their delicate perfume wafted in the breeze.

In two days, the next B&B guests would arrive.

Three generations of the Cooper family were coming to the Côte d'Azur on an emotional journey. Linda Cooper had explained the reason for their visit to Katherine when she wrote to enquire about staying at the Villa des Violettes.

My father-in-law, Tom Cooper, is a hearty ninety-three years old. He helped to liberate the south of France in 1944 at the age of 18 when he arrived with an American Infantry Division. They landed at Camel Beach near St. Raphael and made their way along the coast through Cannes and Nice. His division arrived in Nice two days after the Niçois resistants liberated the city in a daring operation. He and one of the young French fighters became friends and this connection has lasted to this day. Miraculously, both men are still in good health and would like to meet again.

Tom has been talking for a while about making one last trip to France with his whole family. So we decided to make his wish come true this year. He and his wife, Mildred, have been to France twice before. This time they want to share the experience with all of us. We will visit Normandy for a week and then arrive in Antibes to stay for a week.

There will be six of us: Tom, Mildred (a much younger 83!), my husband Clayton and me, and our two daughters, Alisha (24) and Carmen (22). We would like to book your three guestrooms.

"*Mon Dieu,*" Philippe had said when Katherine showed

him Linda's message. "It will be a pleasure to have this family stay with us. We must do everything we can to help them."

Katherine was well aware of how grateful the people of France still were to the men who had liberated the country from the German occupation. In each town, the anniversary of the most significant dates was recognized with a respectful ceremony.

"Two more days and you will have your *aubergiste* hat on again, ma belle. Are you ready for this?"

"*Tout à fait!* Absolutely! Especially since we have Lucille to help out. I wouldn't be able to manage without her!"

Katherine and Philippe were waiting on the front steps when Bernadette pulled into the driveway, this time in her large van.

The Cooper family climbed out and Bernadette unloaded the luggage. Clayton offered to help but was quickly and politely chastised. Philippe chuckled as he shook his hand, "Now you know why we always do exactly what Bernadette says."

Katherine greeted everyone by name and with a *bise*. "Since Linda wrote to us about your family, we feel like we already know you. Come in and I will show you your rooms. Are you tired from your trip?"

Linda glanced at the rest of the family then said, "We are actually quite well rested as we took the TGV from Paris. More than a few of us snoozed most of the way down."

"Until we reached the coast," Carmen said, her eyes bright with excitement. "Once we saw the turquoise sea, we didn't want to miss a thing."

Alisha joined in, "Gramps told us stories as the train took us along the coast at St. Raphael. It's the first time that he has talked to us about his war experience here. I've been taking notes so I can write a journal for my family."

"Good for you," Philippe said. "Those stories need to be remembered."

"I can second that," Kat said, thinking about how her own mother's stories about the war were almost lost forever.

Kat showed the Coopers their rooms and told them not to hesitate to ask any questions or request help. "We are here to make your stay as wonderful as possible." Then she invited them to join her and Philippe in the salon for a glass of wine. She checked to make certain there were no problems with allergies and with the family's encouragement brought the dogs and kittens in.

"We have pets at home so this suits us perfectly," Linda said, as Philippe poured her a glass of rosé. Carmen and Alisha settled on the floor to play with the dogs and cuddle the kittens.

Kat made a mental note that the pets were true icebreakers. Within no time, everyone was chatting and relaxed. The girls wanted to know about clubs in the area for a little evening action. Linda and her mother-in-law were interested in shopping, and Kat showed them, on maps, the locations of the markets and the good shopping streets in Antibes and Nice.

Linda told Katherine, "Clayton and I visited Nice with Mom and Dad before the girls were born. That tells you how long it has been! It's amazing how the years have flown. We often talked about returning, but having children changes everything, doesn't it? We had to start saving for college instead of travel."

Clayton and Tom were mesmerized by the story Philippe

was telling them about a British submarine secretly coming into the Baie de la Salis in 1942 to deliver communications equipment to the Resistance here. "It happened just down at the bottom of our street. In fact, come into the garden with me and I will show you precisely where it arrived and where the memorial is. I can arrange for Bernadette to take you to see it, if you'd like."

He also promised to email them a link to an excellent local blog that detailed the history of the clandestine operation. "Bernadette can drive you to the places of historical importance, wherever you wish to go. She is a veritable encyclopedia, particularly about the history of the Second World War," he said.

"One never knows what secrets and stories there still are in the villages and towns along the coast and throughout France," Tom said. "We learned so much in the week we just spent in Normandy. I lost my brother there on D-Day."

"My condolences," Philippe offered solemnly. "War is such tragedy." He felt awkward for making such a trite remark, as heartfelt as it was.

Tom explained that he and Mildred had come to the south of France as newlyweds. "We reconnected with Pascal, who was in the Resistance in Nice and had befriended me, and he introduced us to his entire family. We will never forget the time we spent with them and their stories about the Occupation. Like most citizens, they had suffered terribly during those years. They had risked everything to hide their Jewish neighbors and friends from the Gestapo. Their bravery and determination is something we usually only see in movies. That year Mildred and I also went to Normandy and found my brother John's grave."

Mildred had joined in the conversation by this time. "That trip was probably the most emotional time of my life.

I cried every day. It was so important to us and even more so to Tom's parents."

Clayton nodded. "A few years after Linda and I were married," he said, "we came to the south of France with Mom and Dad and camped all along the coast. We met Pascal's family then and spent many happy hours with them. We are so glad that he is still alive and that we will all get to see him in Nice."

Tom said, "Even though I have not talked much about those days with my family, and particularly not with our granddaughters, lately I've been feeling a growing desire for them to understand what I and others who served went through."

Katherine was touched by the emotion she could see on all their faces as Tom spoke. She was reminded of her trip with her nephew to her mother's former village in Ukraine and the meaningful, although painful, experience that was.

Linda suggested they should get organized in their rooms and then go out for a meal. She had already made reservations at a restaurant they remembered from their visit all those years ago, and had arranged for Bernadette to pick them up at 7:00 p.m.

"Then we will see you all at breakfast," Kat said. "I will be in the kitchen by 7:30."

Before she went to bed that night, Kat set the guests' breakfast table, then she and Philippe went outside while Rocco and Coco had one last run around.

"*Minou*, I think you are a natural at this innkeeping business. You seem to be quite calm this time."

"I'm in a much better frame of mind. When our first guests were here, I was consumed with worry for Delphine. I'm surprised I was able to string any intelligent sentences together," Kat said.

"*Malgré cela*, you were a gracious and helpful host, and the Kingsburys clearly enjoyed their stay here. I believe you were to the *auberge* born!"

Kat snorted. "Thank you, *Chouchou*. Your encouragement helps. We will see how well we do as time goes by. We are going to have a full house for most of the summer, except for the one-week break each month you advised me to schedule. Let's hope this visit goes well."

By the end of the Coopers' stay, Katherine and Philippe were reassured not only that their bed and breakfast venture was going to work practically, but also that they liked having guests.

Each morning, warm madeleines and fresh croissants were already on the island when Kat came into the kitchen. She discovered that she enjoyed preparing breakfast for their guests and being invited to join in their conversation. She loved telling them about the wonderful places to visit along the Côte d'Azur that few tourist guides ever mentioned.

Bernadette became a frequent visitor too, coming often to pick up the Coopers and take them to their destination. She mentioned to Kat that she appreciated the additional income this brought her.

Lucille turned out to be a dependable helper. She arrived by 9:00 each morning, prepared to do whatever was required of her, from making beds to scrubbing floors. She took pride in doing housework, and Katherine was pleased with the results.

"*L'esprit d'équipe*. Teamwork." Philippe said as they talked about it over dinner after the Coopers had departed. "You've got it working!"

Kat nodded. "You're part of the team, *Chouchou*. We need your support and encouragement! But the best part, no question, is the lovely friendship offered by our guests—so far anyway. With our first two bookings, our guests have become almost like family. I'm surprised at how personal our conversations have been. The stories I have heard prove to me that most people are good and kind—and interesting!"

Philippe smiled. "*Tu vois, ma chérie, ça va dans les deux sens.* It works both ways."

22

"I can't believe the traffic was so light," Kat remarked as Philippe brought the Ducati to a stop by the vehicle loading area on the dock in Nice. The line of cars snaked well past the dock, but the separate line for motorcycles had only a dozen ahead of them.

"Midday is the best time to avoid rush hour in Nice," Philippe said.

The ferry to Corsica was dockside, looking jaunty in its fresh yellow and white coat of paint. A sign indicated boarding would commence in fifteen minutes.

A horn honked lightly, not too far from them. They turned and saw Bernadette just behind the pedestrian fence, with their luggage at her feet.

"You stay here with the bike, please, and I'll get the bags from Bernadette," Kat said. "They aren't that heavy."

When Kat and Philippe had planned their week-long getaway to Corsica, she thought they would take only what could be packed on the motorcycle. But later, Philippe changed the plan slightly and said he had made arrangements for a van driver to take their luggage on to each place where they would be staying. Kat had been keen to pack lightly, but she acquiesced and added more at Philippe's suggestion. She was not certain how the arrangement would work, but Philippe was adamant he knew what he was doing, and she trusted his judgement.

Once everything was loaded and secured on the bike and they had driven on board, they went up to the lounge in the ferry's bow and found two comfortable seats. Leaving their jackets and some books on them in the hope no one would take the seats, they went outside so Katherine could photograph the boat leaving the mainland. It would be a new perspective of Nice for her.

"Okay, I've taken enough shots and I'm starting to get a bit chilly," Kat said after the city slipped below the horizon.

"*D'accord!* There's nothing to see until the island comes into view in a couple of hours," Philippe said. "Then you won't be able to control yourself. *Je t'assure. C'est magnifique!*"

Two hours later, Kat felt a nudge and opened her eyes. She noticed her eReader in her lap and realized she had been dozing.

"Time to wake up, *Minou*," Philippe said. "You won't want to miss seeing the island come into view."

The sea was smooth and the day clear—perfect conditions for landscape photography. Kat pulled out her camera and started shooting as soon as the craggy silhouettes of the mountains reared up against the cloudless blue sky. "If every view is going to be like this, it is going to be difficult to stop shooting. How spectacular!"

The town of Bastia gleamed golden in the afternoon sun as the ferry docked in the new port. The twin bell towers of what Philippe said was the Church of St. John the Baptist stood out against the hills and mountains behind.

"Let's check into our hotel. Then we can explore the town a bit and grab some dinner. The old port is where we want to be," Philippe said.

By the time they found the hotel and unpacked what they needed for the evening, the sun was low in the sky and it was starting to feel cool. Katherine was glad she had brought a warm shawl. She wrapped it around her neck now, certain it would come in handy after sunset.

They strolled toward the old port along narrow, cobbled streets lined with crumbling buildings, most of them evidently centuries old and in a mix of Italian and French styles. Kat found them charming. Their peeling facades in shades of ochre, salmon and gold seemed to her to promise fascinating stories about their histories.

It was too early in the season for there to be many tourists, and as they walked, they heard the local Corsu dialect more often than any other language. Cheerful birdsong was coming from cages in the gardens and on the balconies of once-grand homes and in the windows of tumbledown tenements.

When they stopped at a bar in the main square to taste the local chestnut beer, Kat said, "I know we are here for the bike trip and the scenery, but let's plan to come back and spend more time in this town. The churches alone look amazing."

Philippe nodded. "It's so easy to get here, we must. I'd forgotten how intriguing it is, and obviously Napoleon is a favored son."

They explored some of the winding laneways around the imposing fifteenth-century *citadel* before going to the *vieux port* area. A quaint bistro on the lively Quai des

Martyrs de la Liberation caught their attention, and they decided to stop there for dinner.

When it was served, Philippe praised his enormous bowl of *aziminu*. "It's the Corsican bouillabaise. *Delicieux!*"

He laughed as Kat looked quickly away from the fish eyes staring out at her from the bowl. She had still not become a convert to bouillabaise. Instead she dug into a spicy shrimp dish and ordered a bowl of chestnut ice cream for dessert. "Two spoons, please."

Early the next morning, stretching exercises were the first order of the day. Then, after a hearty breakfast, they donned their leather motorcycle gear and were soon on a back road heading south to the western coast.

They had two destinations for the day. One was a requisite visit to a goat-cheese farm. Katherine had laughed when Philippe first mentioned it. "On a trip with you, how could there not be a visit to a cheese producer?"

The other, more important, stop was the small village where they planned to spread Simone's son's ashes, as she had requested.

"I'm so glad we can do this for Simone," Kat said, as they chatted through their headsets. "I feel sad thinking about how long she held that wish in her heart and yet could not bring herself to come here."

"We should be there by late morning," Philippe said, glancing at the GPS on his instrument panel. "It's not nearly as inaccessible today as it was seventy years ago, as you might imagine."

The ride there was exhilarating. They climbed vertiginous roads that twisted up hills covered with wild maquis, the dense aromatic shrubbery that so defined Corsica. They wound through forests of chestnut trees, leaned into spine-tingling hairpin curves and swept down heart-stopping descents toward stunning sapphire bays glistening in the sun. The twitters and whistles of birds and the heavily-scented air added to the heady sense of being surrounded by the best of nature's bounty. There were times Katherine felt overwhelmed by it all. None more so than when they stopped in the afternoon and followed a footpath from the square of a tiny hamlet to find the house where Simone had given birth to Jean-Luc.

Simone's directions had been clear. The humble cottage stood precisely where she had described. The elderly grandson of her aunt lived there now. He smiled warmly as he welcomed them, saying Simone had written to him in advance. He invited them in to the simple kitchen and offered a glass of chestnut beer. As they chatted, he described how the story of Simone's time in the village had been passed down the generations. After rummaging in an old armoire, he brought out a small box of stained, sepia photos.

"All these decades later, it is still easy to recognize that beautiful young woman as Simone," Kat said. The grandson insisted they take the photos to her, and Kat thanked him profusely, knowing how pleased Simone would be to see them.

After they said their goodbyes to the old man, Kat and Philippe walked down a path through the maquis covering the hillside and perfuming the air with mint, lavender, rosemary and other aromas Kat couldn't quite identify.

"Simone told me Corsica was called the Scented Isle as well as the Beautiful Isle," Katherine said, her voice low and soft. "I can see why. And I can see why she loved it so."

They stopped in a clearing where the view over the valleys to the sea was breathtaking. Kat took several shots after deciding to make a small photo album of them as a gift to Simone. She also gathered a bouquet of plants to dry and keep as a lasting reminder of this trip. Then they gently scattered Jean-Luc's ashes over the surrounding maquis. Philippe read a poem in French, given to him by Simone for the occasion. The quiet moment perfectly suited the serenity and beauty of the setting.

For a while, they sat together on the slope, leaning against each other and feeling the visceral connection that bound them. Philippe translated the poem for Kat as best he could, and they talked about how Simone and the infant Jean-Luc may have passed their time in this very spot. From time to time, Philippe brushed his fingers through Kat's hair and across the back of her neck. She nestled her head on his shoulder, her hand on his thigh.

"And then her lover, Gregoire, finally traced them to this remote place and stayed with them," Kat said. "Imagine how that passionate reunion played out in this exquisite setting." Her voice became tremulous, not much more than a whisper. "Such a love story."

Philippe nodded. "I feel honored Simone chose to share that story with us. And to think that, in fact, Jean-Luc was my uncle ... *incroyable.*"

Silently, they shed tears for their dear friend whose life had been altered here so very long ago.

---

23

*A*fter a thrilling ride down to the coast, they stopped for a quick lunch at a bistro by the sea. It turned into what Philippe described as *une vraie experience gastronomique*. The menu featured langoustine, and Kat and Philippe were soon sharing a gigantic platter of the glistening pink crustaceans. They looked to Kat like a cross between a lobster and a large shrimp, and she asked Philippe why they were considered such a delicacy.

"They would be ridiculously expensive anywhere else," Philippe explained. "They must be eaten right after they are killed because their meat begins to deteriorate immediately. Shipping them still alive is what makes them so expensive elsewhere, but they thrive in the sea here. These were no doubt caught this morning. This is a true bonanza!" He grinned and flourished his large white napkin.

The waiter brought them both finger bowls, and soon Katherine was tearing into the meal with both hands and as much enthusiasm as Philippe.

"These are incredibly delicious," she mumbled through a mouthful.

An hour later they were back on the Ducati, their appetites thoroughly sated. Their route took them inland through the scrubby Desert des Agriates.

"The guide book says it's the only official desert in Europe," Kat said. "It sure doesn't look like a desert to me though."

They stopped several times so Kat could photograph the endless maquis-covered hills and valleys, each time exclaiming over the perfumed air. At times the view was of a line of barren summits and at others the wild and rocky hill-sides tumbled down to long beaches of white sand lapped by the sparkling turquoise sea. Occasionally, they caught sight of one of the iconic Genoese watchtowers built 500 years ago to keep pirates and invading forces at bay.

In the late afternoon, they reached the beach town of Ile Rousse, which offered stunning views of a red rock island not far offshore. Kat climbed off the motorcycle and stretched, saying, "Ouch! I need a yoga session and a good hot bath. I hadn't thought about what it would be like to ride on that bike for eight hours, especially when I'm hanging on for dear life half the time!"

Philippe tousled Kat's hair as she took off her helmet. "*D'accord! C'est dur*. It's not so easy when we are out of practice."

"But it's worth the pain just to see this amazing scenery. What a beautiful island!" Kat said, her eyes bright. "When we came around some of those corners, the view was almost intoxicating."

"*Tu n'as encore rien vu*. What's that saying in English that you taught me?" Philippe asked.

Kat laughed. "You ain't seen nothin' yet."

Philippe nodded. "*Attends un peu!* Just you wait!"

As Philippe had promised, their luggage had arrived at

the hotel before them and was left in their room. The space was small but, to compensate, it had a large window overlooking the harbor.

Kat checked out the en-suite bathroom before joining Philippe at the window. "The view is wonderful, *mon chou*, but the best part is the deep bath tub! How did you manage that?"

Philippe went for a stroll to check out dining spots, while Kat did her yoga exercises to loosen her tight muscles. Then she soaked herself in a hot bath. By the time Philippe returned, Kat was ready for something to eat.

"I found a place that serves what might be the most impressive charcuterie platter ever." Philippe announced. "*Formidable!* It has to be seen to be believed."

They stopped along the way to the restaurant to enjoy the last dying rays of the sunset. Once again, Katherine was glad to have a shawl to wrap around her shoulders.

The small room they entered from the street turned out to be only the foyer to the restaurant. They were led straight through it and out the back door into a narrow alley set with long wooden tables. Several people were already seated, and the air was abuzz with conversation and laughter. Propane heaters were warming the cool night air.

"Charcuterie is Corsica's signature dish," Philippe told Kat, as the waiter poured them a dry, full-bodied local red wine to complement their meal. "Although there is plenty of seafood, the real stars of Corsican cuisine are meats like wild boar and pork from maquis-fed pigs, and local cheeses, honey and chestnuts."

Soon a large wooden platter arrived heaped so high it made Kat gasp. "I feel like we should be sharing this with the entire table," Kat whispered to Philippe, who pointed out that most couples were also sharing a similar meal. The *planche* was overflowing with thinly sliced prosciutto, salami and smoked wild boar along with olives, three different cheeses and a small pot of fig jam.

Philippe explained the different local cheeses, saying that everything would have a touch of the maquis in one way or another. His eyes lit up as he told her about *brocciu*.

"I would say it is the most treasured ingredient of Corsican chefs. It's richer than the creamiest ricotta and is used in many of the island's favorite dishes. Just taste this. We're going to stop in at a dairy farm farther south. I can't wait to show you!"

At the end of each table sat a small plate with slivers of meat and drops of honey. The waiter explained that they were "bee plates"—an invitation for bees to enjoy themselves there rather than buzz around other plates. Now that it was after dark, there were no bees around to demonstrate, but Kat made a mental note to remember this for meals on the terrace at the villa.

Dessert was *falculella,* Corsican cheesecake, made with *brocciu* and baked on chestnut leaves. Its contrast of flavors was, Kat declared, "irresistible" and it left both of them smiling contentedly as they strolled back to their hotel.

24

"Today is going to be our longest ride," Philippe said after breakfast as they were putting on their gear and preparing to leave. "But you will be blown away by what we see, I promise. I'm glad I reminded you to charge your camera battery last night. Your shutter is going to be steaming today!"

"I can't believe it will be better than where we've already been," Kat said.

"Not necessarily better, but different. It's a particularly special area."

Before they left, they both took a few minutes to send texts and check that all was in order back home.

Simone replied with a heartfelt message of appreciation for the photos Kat sent.

Delphine reported that all the pets were doing fine and everything was under control. Kat's eyes twinkled as she read the message to Philippe, "Alfonso drops by every evening to see if there is anything he can do to help. We go for walks with the dogs and talk about everything."

"I don't want to read too much into it," Kat said, "but I am hopeful."

Gilles sent Philippe a report from the market that made him laugh. "He says he is enjoying the calm before the storm when the tourists start arriving after Easter and that we should stay away longer!"

Philippe spent the next ten minutes texting back and forth with Gilles. He said they were discussing a few supply and scheduling issues. Kat was happy to use the time to edit a few photos.

Soon they were on their way, following the coastline for a while and riding through air perfumed by the maquis. Then, after a long climb up a hillside, the landscape changed in the blink of an eye, or so it seemed to Kat. Suddenly, towering volcanic pinnacles came into view, and on one side the road was crowded by a jagged rock wall of deep red, pink and ochre and on the other by a sheer drop to the shimmering sea. The water in the numerous inlets they passed was a shade of intense, deep blue Kat tried to but couldn't name. She was speechless with excitement. Whenever it was safe to pull off the road, they did, and Kat took many photos.

"Wow—just wow! As you said—fantastic!" she exclaimed repeatedly.

"These inlets are called *calanches*, like our *calanques* at home. And this area is a UNESCO World Heritage Site. We will go to the Scandola Nature Preserve while we're here too. *En fait*, let's go down to the marina in Porto and see about reserving seats on a boat tour."

As they stood on one overhang, safely off the road, Kat took Philippe's hand and pulled him close. Their lips met in a kiss neither wanted to end, and their arms encircled each other. "Thank you for bringing me here," she murmured at last.

Philippe looked into her eyes. "We have a way of making beautiful memories, *Minou*. And we will keep doing it. There's so much more to discover together."

They found a spot to sit and absorbed the extraordinary scenery for quite a while, mostly in silence. Then, helmets and headsets back in place, they began the thrilling descent to the shore.

~

They had no problem finding the marina in the village of Porto. There were quite a few boats of all sizes: local fishing boats, tour boats and private yachts. Katherine commented on the size of some of them.

Philippe gestured toward a nearby bar and suggested they stop for a beer before booking their seats. "I'm feeling quite parched after that ride!" he said, and Kat suddenly realized how thirsty she was.

They found a table overlooking the water and sat quietly, sipping their beers and admiring the view. Kat closed her eyes to enjoy the warmth of the sun on her face. Moments later, she heard a familiar voice saying. "*Pardon-nez-moi*, but is this seat taken?"

Her eyes flew open and she felt glued to her chair she was so stunned. "Nick! Oh my God! Nick! Niiiiiick!" Her eyes flashed to Philippe, who was looking at her and grinning from ear to ear, and back to their Australian friend, who was also grinning broadly. Then she leapt into Nick's waiting arms. "What on earth are you doing here?"

After a long, rocking hug with Kat, Nick shook Philippe's

hand, then the two men *bised* and embraced as great friends do. They were both laughing.

"What? How?" Kat sputtered, staring wide-eyed at their tall, tanned friend, with sunglasses perched on his close-cropped silvery hair. *He's as handsome as ever*, she thought.

They all sat down, and after Philippe ordered Nick a beer he explained to Kat that they had planned this rendezvous months ago. Nick had picked up his new yacht in Marseille a few weeks earlier. With his steadfast captain, Tim, and Tim's wife, Twig, who took care of managing everything on Nick's yachts, plus three other new crew members, they had sailed to Corsica.

As Kat's thoughts settled, she reminded herself how this was part of Nick's modus operandi. He had a habit of turning up at the most surprising and unexpected times. There was that time in Marseille. Then in Toronto, and the wedding in Antibes.

Nicholas Field was an exceedingly wealthy man, thanks to a clever early entry in the high-tech business and the sale of his business some years later. He spent much of his current life on his luxurious yacht, when he was not flying somewhere in his private jet. He devoted a great deal of time directing his charitable foundation, which quietly provided assistance to under-served communities in many parts of the world.

The other side to Nick was his kindness, generosity and loyalty to friends. He loved life, and to him that also meant sharing his good fortune with those friends. Since Kat and Philippe first met him in Antibes, they had experienced his generous nature several times, most notably when he flew all of Kat's family and friends from Toronto to Antibes for her wedding to Philippe. That had been a complete surprise, never to be forgotten.

Kat's gaze settled on Nick now and she could not stop smiling.

He flashed a dazzling grin back and winked. "I have two other guests on the boat. You will love them. So there will be five passengers on *Searendipity II.*"

"I still don't understand," Kat said.

"We're getting on Nick's yacht here," Philippe explained, "and cruising around the island for another week. We can get off and go on the bike when and wherever we want or simply enjoy life on the boat. We've got several great stops planned."

Kat sprang up from her chair and hugged first Nick and then Philippe. "This is simply unreal! How wonderful! Most of all it is just wonderful to see you, Nick. You told us you were coming back to Antibes this summer, but this is an unbelievable surprise. You've done it to us again!"

They settled back into their chairs and toasted their friendship with their chilled beers. After chatting for a few minutes, Nick looked past Katherine and said, "Here come my other two passengers. I'll get them to join us."

When Katherine turned to look, a man and a woman were standing directly behind her. Kat screamed so loudly, everyone in earshot peered at her to see what was going on.

"Molly! Tony! No! This is just too much! It's impossible!" And she burst into tears as they all wrapped their arms around each other. Then Kat and Molly hugged each other and jumped up and down together, squealing and crying. The three men looked on in amusement.

When the two women settled down at last, more explanations followed.

Philippe took Kat's hand and said, "You know that Nick and I keep in contact with each other. And, as you said, you knew that Nick was coming to Antibes this spring in his new boat. We were emailing each other all through the worri-some days when Delphine was missing—"

Nick raised his hand. "Let me interrupt here, *mon ami*. Philippe let me know how distraught you were, Kat. We had been talking about when I planned to arrive in Antibes, probably in late May. Then we had the idea of meeting up here and cruising around the island for a few days. After that I talked to Molly and Tony to see if I could get them here too."

Philippe nodded. "What better tonic for you, Kat? We decided to go ahead with this anyway, even after Delphine came back."

Molly said, "An even happier ending to a happy ending! Not bad, eh, Katski?"

As the conversation continued, more details came out. Tony explained that, through his ministry in Toronto, he had been invited to a large Anglican synod in London. "And it is happening in ten days, so I was able to tie in our trip here with that."

Molly added, "I arranged a leave of absence from school and—badda bing, badda boom—here we are! If you like, I'll go back to the Cap with you guys, and Tony will come there from his meetings for a couple of days before we fly back to Toronto. How does that sound?"

"If we like? Are you crazy? Awesome! Unbelievable! I'm speechless ..." Kat's voice trailed off and she slowly shook her head. Her heart was overflowing.

Philippe said, "Here's the plan. Nick will anchor in Ajaccio while you meet André and go to the landscape course. You can do that and then come back on the boat for two more days before we go home. Tony will fly to London from here, and you, Molly and I will fly to Nice. Nick will stay on in Corsica for a while and will bring the Ducati back to Antibes with him. How's that for organization?"

"And now," Nick announced, "I've reserved seats for us on a tour boat that will take us to the Scandola Nature Reserve this afternoon. Boats the size of *Searendipity* aren't allowed in. We've got a lot of adventures ahead of us this week."

"*On y va!*" Philippe said, and they all leaped to their feet. "Let's get this show on the road!"

25

*B*ernadette was waiting at the airport in Nice the morning that Molly, Kat and Philippe arrived back from Corsica. Bangles jingled on her arm as she gave each of them a *bise*. She greeted Molly like a long lost friend. "*Quelle surprise!* I did not know you were *en Corse* wiz les Dufours! Et Monsieur Tony?"

Kat said, "It was a grand surprise for me too! Philippe arranged it. They were waiting there on Nick's new yacht."

"*Oh là là!* Monsieur Nicholas." Bernadette paused for a second, and her face took on a dreamy expression. "Now zere eez a fine man! 'E eez coming too?"

Laughing, Philippe said, "*Sois patiente!* Patience! Tony is coming in a few days, and Nick will probably be here in June."

This set Bernadette off on one of her rants about the dearth of good men to be found in France. Philippe opened the back of the van and went to put the luggage in, but Bernadette, her rant over, stopped him. Handling the baggage was part of her job, and she was determined to do it alone.

As she drove along the Bord de Mer, she updated her passengers in her colorful manner on the local gossip. Philippe paid polite attention, but at their first chance, Molly and Kat started chattering. Once they were driving along the streets leading to the Cap, Molly kept exclaiming, breathless with excitement, each time she recognized a favorite spot. She hugged Katherine several times, and the two friends grinned wordlessly at each other.

Before long, Bernadette pulled the van up at the front door of the Villa des Violettes. In the ten days they had been gone, the flowering trees and shrubs had exploded into bloom and spring flowers carpeted the perennial beds bordering the lawn.

"Wow!" Molly exclaimed. "Everything looks fabulous. I'm so excited to be back here."

Katherine's face was shining with delight. "And we are so excited to have you back here!"

"Look at all the lily of the valley in the woods," Molly said. "That was so cool of Nick to have bouquets of them in our cabins on the first of May. I love that tradition here."

She was referring to the *fête du muguet*, held every May 1st, when the French give sprigs of the fragrant flower to their close friends.

Bernadette had all the van doors open and was again telling everyone not to touch any luggage. She was looking pointedly at Philippe, who chuckled and unloaded some of the bags anyway. "*Calme-toi, mon amie!*" he said. "You can't keep bossing me around. I'm going to help you, and that's that! *C'est ça!*"

Laden with suitcases and backpacks, the two of them disappeared into the house. Just as quickly, Bernadette was back outside saying goodbye. Molly and Kat waved as she drove off and then they turned to walk into the house.

"Holy shmoly!" Molly stopped at the front door and stared at the wisteria that framed it. The vine was covered in a cascade of purple blossoms. "Talk about wisteria hysteria," she gasped, breathing in the sweet scent. "That's dazzling! I don't remember this from last year."

"You're right," Kat agreed. "It hardly bloomed at all last year. Auguste claims it was waiting for the villa to be filled with love again. He swears plants feel these things."

"He may be on to something there because this is one hell of a happy looking vine," Molly said. Looking around, she added, "And the flower beds look downright ecstatic!"

Belle appeared from behind a large terra cotta pot and wound around Kat's legs.

"Belle!" Molly squealed, reaching down to pet her. "I can't wait to see the kittens and—"

She was interrupted by Coco and Rocco barreling out the front door and bouncing around them. Delphine followed right behind them.

"*Bienvenue chez vous*! Welcome home!" She greeted them. "As you can see, you were missed."

Katherine gave Delphine an affectionate *bise* before Molly excitedly threw her arms around the young woman. "Oops! *Excusez-moi*! I know I'm not supposed to hug in France but I can't help it seeing you. We were so worried and I'm so glad you are safely back."

Delpine smiled and graciously responded to Molly's hug. "Katherine told me you and Tony kept me in your prayers. *Merci mille fois*."

In the meantime Kat was trying to get the dogs to sit, and they obeyed with evident difficulty. Their tails wagged frantically and their eyes shifted excitedly between the two women. Following a hand signal from Delphine, they stayed sitting while Molly knelt down and petted them both. The dogs wiggled excitedly and, after another hand signal, dashed off down the lawn running circles around each other.

"Wow!" Kat said to Delphine, "you must teach me that command."

"I'm impressed by how well-trained they are!" Molly said.

"Ha! It's still hit or miss whether they obey me or not. Delphine has the magic touch," Kat replied with a wry expression. "Once they've run off a little energy, they will probably shadow you for the rest of the day."

Molly was anxious to see all the changes Kat and Philippe had made to the villa, and after they took her for a complete walk-through, she exclaimed, "I can't believe how much has been accomplished in just a year. I don't know how you did it."

Their smiles displayed their pride. "Honestly, Moll," Kat said, "it was teamwork all the way—and a lot of luck! The only real problem we had was with the Roman ruins that were found where we wanted to put the parking spaces. But that is all settled now."

Philippe explained, "While that slowed down work outside, we were able to finish up a lot of things inside. It gave us the time to take care of a lot of details. Didier and his crew worked miracles."

"I can't wait to see those guys again," Molly said. "They turned the villa into a magical place for your wedding reception. They and that great group of Adorée's friends. I'll never forget that."

As they put together a light lunch, they reminisced about the wedding. "What coincidental timing! Once Tony arrives the day after tomorrow, we will all be together again for our first anniversary on May 5," Kat said. Noticing the sly look Molly and Philippe exchanged, she continued, "Hmmm—or maybe somebody planned all this."

Philippe grinned, and Kat threw her arms around him. "You and your surprises! *Je t'adore!*"

After lunch, Philippe suggested that they go to see Simone. "I'm sure she is waiting to hear about our pilgrimage to her aunt's village. Even though you sent her a lot of photos, Kat, we should talk to her."

"Yes, of course, and before we do anything else," Kat replied.

"I will wait here for a while," Molly suggested. "This will be a very intimate conversation. Just text me when I should come over."

"Good thinking, Moll. Thanks for being so considerate about it," Kat said. "I'll go and get the maquis I collected for Simone."

Molly smiled. "It will be nice to spend time with her again. She left such an impression on me last year. Ninety-frickin-five, right? Sheesh! I brought her a little something from Canada, so I'll go unpack and wait to hear from you."

Katherine held Philippe's hand as they walked along the path to Simone's. "I'm really going to have to work at not crying. You know me ..."

Philippe squeezed her hand. "*Ne t'inquiète pas, Minou.* Don't worry. If you cry, you cry. It's a sad situation. I am just so glad you and I were able to carry out her wish."

Kat's eyes widened as they neared Simone's villa. A blaze of purple blossoms arched across the path from the front garden to where the vine was anchored on the wall over the front door. "Look at that bougainvillea! In the time we were gone it has burst into flower. Wow!"

"Isn't it spectacular?" Simone asked, standing in the open doorway. "I saw you coming through the window—not that I was looking." She gave them both a lingering *bise* and invited them inside. "Let us sit in the salon. I have a *tarte aux fraises* just out of the oven waiting for us. *Un petit goût!*"

Simone chose her favorite chair by the window, and Katherine and Philippe sat across from her on the sofa.

"*Dites-moi tout.* I want to hear everything," Simone said.

Kat swallowed hard. The memory of those moments on the Corsican hillside were etched deeply in her heart. But she found her voice and began to tell the story of what she and Philippe had done with the ashes. Simone's serenity gave her the strength to carry on without halting. When Kat had finished, Simone smiled in gratitude. "Since you sent those stunning photos of the morning you let Jean-Luc's spirit free, a weight has lifted inside me. Those were a beautiful few years we spent there, the early days when it was just me with my sweet baby and then those after Gregoire found us. I believe there is no greater loss for a mother than that of her child. Her heart is shattered into a million pieces. She spends the rest of her life trying to put it back together. I wonder if it ever can be mended?"

Simone's voice was hushed. Katherine felt tears well and closed her eyes briefly.

"And the answer to that," Simone continued, "is no. *Jamais.* Never. However, I have learned through the years that it is possible to feel alive again. To feel joy. To see the good in life after you feel you never will again. This simple act you carried out for me has put more of those million pieces back together in my heart, and I am more at peace than before. I can never thank you enough."

She rose from her chair and sat between Kat and Philippe. She took one of their hands in each of hers. They sat silently for several minutes, then Simone patted their hands. No further words were necessary.

"*Et bien*," Simone said, breaking the silence in a strong, clear voice. "Now where is our dear Molly? Thank you for texting me about the surprise. What a joy!"

Katherine looked at Philippe. Her eyes pleaded with him to step in and give her another minute to pull herself together. She wanted to find some of Simone's inner strength.

"Molly is waiting at the villa," Philippe replied. "She is so looking forward to seeing you. I will text her right now."

Simone was still holding Kat's hand. She lifted it to her lips and kissed the back of it. "*Ça va, ma chérie. Je vais bien.* I am fine, darling Kat." Then she stood and beckoned Kat. "Come, let's put the water on for tea."

Katherine smiled weakly and took in a big breath as she stood up. "You are my hero, Simone. *Tu es vraiment mon inspiration.*"

26

*T*he next afternoon, Katherine and Molly hiked the rugged Sentier du Littoral, the path that follows the southern coast of the Cap. The sun was high in a clear blue sky, the breeze was light and the sea glittered in dazzling shades of azure. On one side of the trail in some places, high stone walls marked the end of private properties, on the other, rocks tumbled down to the glittering sea. Much of the greenery along the path was alive with splashes of bright pink Daphne, dainty wild daisies, and patches of golden broom.

"Some of this is just like the maquis in Corsica, right?" Molly said.

"Yes, not nearly as intense though. Don't you love the perfect weather I arranged for us?" Kat kidded.

"I feel like we're walking through a frickin' movie set," Molly whooped and did a little dance on the narrow path. She threw her arms wide, gesturing to the rolling hills and snow-capped Alps in the distance, across the water.

They paused so often to soak in the sun and the view and for Kat to take photographs it took them two hours to walk the trail. When the end came in sight, they decided on one final rest stop and settled on a large rock on the shore.

"I don't want the trail to finish," Molly sighed and Kat agreed. A light spray of salt water blew over them.

"Oh, that is refreshing. Bring it on! I'm definitely overheating." Molly exclaimed. "My hair is out of control." She pulled back her mass of wild black curls and secured them with a hair tie.

"Me too," Kat said, wiping her brow. "We should have walked this earlier in the morning, but that rain shower got in the way."

"I'm so glad it cleared up," Molly said. "Remember when we walked the trail the first time we came to Antibes together, Katski?"

Kat grinned and nodded. "How could I forget? In some ways it feels like yesterday and, in others, like years, so much has happened to both of us since then. But those days we had together were unforgettable. I'm not certain I have ever laughed more, thanks to you!"

Molly put her arm around Kat's shoulders. "We've been through so much together, girlfriend ... for more than half a frickin' century!" She shouted the last part out over the waves.

Kat laughed. "All the way back to Madame LaChapelle's French immersion kindergarten class."

"If she could only see you now, *parlezing français* like a local," Molly said with a grin. "Who knew?"

They exchanged a glance that conveyed their amusement and amazement, and shook their heads.

"Funny the path life takes us on," Kat said. "But through all the ups and downs along the way, we've always been there for each other. Now here we are, closing in on sixty and both of us happier than we have ever been."

Molly stared out over the water. "There were more than a few times I wasn't sure I would make it through the current crisis," she said, "especially as a kid. But you and your parents always took me in. Your home was my refuge and a reminder that there were people who truly cared about me. Elisabeth was amazing. Best mother ever."

Kat nodded. "I still carry them close in my heart. I wish they could see how our lives are now."

Pointing skyward and twirling her fingers, Molly said, "They're out there somewhere looking down on us. I'm convinced of that."

"Thinking about my mother helped carry me through those horrible weeks when Delphine was missing. There were times when I was losing hope that she would return. Then I'd remember all that Anyu went through when she was about the same age as Delphine, the horrors of the war and hiding from the Gestapo, immigrating to Canada with nothing but her wits. She would always say it was hope that made it happen. Bless her."

"Yup—and of course, her favorite proverb: What doesn't kill us makes us stronger. I never hear those words without thinking of her. I was so happy to see her carpet hanging on the wall in your entryway. Her spirit lives on in so many ways."

"It does," Kat agreed. "Thank goodness for that! And now, my dear bestie, we better get going if we're going to make it home in time for *apéros* with Philippe. I can't wait until Tony gets here tomorrow night."

"Me too! Even more, I can't wait for the day after that. Your first wedding anniversary and the most unusual celebration of it that I've ever heard."

They high-fived and laughed.

27

*O*n the morning of May 5, Katherine wakened to a gentle kiss on her cheek. She breathed in the freshly-showered scent of the man she loved with all her heart. Savoring the cool feel of his damp hair against her skin, she opened her eyes.

"*Joyeux anniversaire, ma douce épouse,*" Philippe whispered in her ear as he sat on the edge of the bed. He grinned as Kat laughed at his rhyming term of endearment

She melted into his strong embrace. "Happy anniversary! *Je t'aime, Chouchou*! The best husband in the world."

"*Pas d'exagération?*" he asked in mock surprise.

"*Pas du tout!* None at all!" Kat replied, feeling just how true that was.

"That was quite the celebration last night!" Philippe said, rolling his eyes.

"I had so much fun! I wish Molly and Tony weren't leaving tomorrow."

"Tony assured me they would come back in the autumn. This is a busy time at work for them both now, but he hinted they may have some surprise news for us in a few months."

"Oh, I wonder what? I'm glad you have the day off," Kat said, stifling a yawn. "When you popped the champagne cork after Tony arrived, I knew we were in trouble. Sleeping in a bit longer than usual this morning is a gift."

"Speaking of gifts, we should get dressed and prepare to receive the gifts Adorée is delivering today. She texted last night that she plans to arrive in time for breakfast."

Kat sat up straight with excitement. "Chickens! It's really happening! And we finally will meet Maxim, her ... um ... friend. We need to remember that, Philippe ... just "*un ami,*" she keeps telling us."

He grinned. They both had a feeling this young man, mentioned by Adorée more times than she was aware, was very close to her heart.

"You see about breakfast, *mon chou*. I bet Molly and Tony are already up. I'll take a quick shower and be right with you."

When Kat came into the kitchen, Molly was setting the table and watching Bonbon and Bijou chase each other around in circles. Their antics culminated in some wild wrestling, which made Molly laugh.

"*Bonjour*, Katski!" Molly greeted Kat with exaggerated *bises*. "These kittens are non-stop entertainment when they aren't sleeping."

"You can see why Belle likes to get out of the house for some peace. They are adorable though, aren't they?" Looking around, Kat asked, "Where are the men?"

Molly pointed out the window. "There seems to be some activity going on at the far end of the potager."

Katherine opened the French doors that led to the

terrace off the kitchen and walked down the four steps to the gate to the fenced garden. Peering through the gate, she could see Philippe, Tony, and Didier and his crew gathered at the *poulailer*.

"Did Philippe say what they were doing?" Kat asked when Molly joined her.

"I guess we will just have to wait to find out," Molly said with a little smile on her face

"They are probably admiring their handiwork once again," Kat said. "Did I tell you that Auguste and Philippe built the hen house? You would have thought they were trying for some architectural prize with all the planning they put into it. But I have to say they did a great job."

In the distance, they heard the sound of a vehicle approaching, then the crunch of tires on the gravel driveway. The two friends ran arm in arm to the back of the villa. A red van pulled up and Adorée hopped down from the passenger side. "*Bonjour tout le monde!*" she greeted every-one. A good-looking, fair-haired young man smiled as he got out from behind the wheel.

The men waved and began walking toward them. Kat and Molly stopped on the terrace, and Adorée brought her companion up the steps with her. "MamaKat and Molly, this is Maxim."

Introductions were made all around when the men arrived, and the air filled with lively conversations in rapid-fire French about the drive, the weather, and the chickens.

"It's a typical early morning French conversation," Kat said to Molly with a chuckle, when she saw her confused look. "I still only ever grasp a snippet."

"Maxim and I agreed on the way down that we should deliver the chickens to their new home before we sit down to breakfast," Adorée said when the chatter died down. "We want to get them out of these crates. We also decided the rooster should come a little later. Is that all right?"

"*Comme tu veux*! Whatever you say!" Kat replied. "You are the chicken queen here."

The men helped unload the wooden boxes with two dozen squawking chickens poking their heads through the slats, and Adorée led the small procession to the hen house.

Kat noticed new window boxes, already planted with flowers, had been installed under the two side windows. She smiled, knowing they must be Auguste's work. A wide red ribbon was stretched across the gate to the fenced-in chicken run.

"*Viens ici*, Kat!" Philippe called, holding out a pair of garden shears. "Come here and cut the ribbon for the official opening."

Everyone applauded as Kat chopped the ribbon. Auguste opened the gate, and Adorée released the chickens. A flurry of brown, white, black and red feathers floated into the air as they flapped and fluffed after their cramped ride. Some then hopped up the ramp to inspect their nesting boxes and roosts. Others began scratching and pecking the ground.

"We gave them some goodies to find. Just a handful or two of wheat and barley grain, " Didier told Katherine, with a wink. "We want you to have happy hens starting right now."

There was a spontaneous chorus of "*Joyeux anniversaire!*" "*Félicitations!*" and finally "*Bonne fête de poulets!*"

"Happy feast of chickens!" Philippe translated for Molly.

She made a face and said, "Yikes! That sounds too much like we're preparing to have them for dinner. Better left untranslated."

Kat explained Molly's comment to Philippe, who in turn

explained it to Didier and crew and they all burst out laughing.

"*Oui*," Philippe agreed. "*C'est mieux en français*. Better in French!"

Molly nudged Kat. "You've got one of those 'I'm so happy I could burst' grins, right now."

"Crazy, isn't it?" Kat said. "But here I am, standing in our revived potager with some of the most special people in my family and cheering about chickens."

"On your first wedding anniversary, no less," Molly added.

"Go figure! I'm so glad you are here for this. After all the worrying revelations of Delphine's experience, it's good to be celebrating with laughter today."

Adorée had moved to stand with them and slipped her arms around Kat's and Molly's shoulders. "You two have the best friendship ever."

"Yes, we do," Kat and Molly replied in unison, with a fist bump.

"Adorée, if there's one lesson you can learn from us it is to choose your friends wisely," Molly said.

"And keep them forever!" Kat added. "No matter what happens in life, always be there for each other. You can't put a value on that."

"I see that every time I watch the two of you ... whether it's on a screen or in the flesh. I'm already learning. Molly, you must come more often to visit!"

"Yes!" Kat said, "Once a year is not enough."

"I'm going to do my best to make that happen," Molly replied. "I can't wait to find out what else is in store at the Villa des Violettes!"

~~~~~~~The End~~~~~~~

COMING NOVEMBER 2019

Watch for Book Three in the *Villa des Violettes* series, coming soon!

AUTHOR'S NOTE

I am SO enjoying being back on the pages with Katherine and Philippe and many other of the characters from my *Love in Provence* series. From the enthusiastic response to *The First Noël at the Villa des Violettes,* (Book One), I'm thrilled to know readers are happy to be there too! It was because of hearing from so many of you that I began the *Villa des Violettes* series. These are slightly shorter reads, not full length novels, and at the moment three are planned. I hope you enjoy following along and spending more time in the south of France.

Thank you to everyone who has written to me through the years or messaged me on social media. I love hearing from readers! I value your thoughts and opinion, so please continue to share them with me at patriciasandsauthor@gmail.com.

Have you signed up for my newsletter? It goes out once a month with all sorts of contests and information about what's coming next. Just click on "<u>subscribe</u>" at my website http://patriciasandsauthor.com/

If you enjoy the photos from France I share online, please <u>follow me on Instagram</u>. I'll be happy to follow you back.

Any time you take a moment to write a review, please know your efforts are appreciated. Comments from readers are helpful and inspiring to me. You are the reason I write and your words encourage others to read my books. *Merci mille fois!* Thanks a million!

And now . . . on to the next book. See you there!

ACKNOWLEDGEMENTS

In order to reach that exciting point where a manuscript is finally ready to publish, a tremendous amount of support and assistance is essential. I'm grateful to everyone who contributed in his or her own personal way to bringing *A Season of Surprises at the Villa des Violettes* to readers.

Friends and family are my rocks. My husband's patient support, encouragement, and critical first look at my words always begin the process.

I appreciate my good fortune to have many advance readers who offer honest, helpful comments and read all my rewrites without losing their sense of humor. Thank you for giving so willingly of your time and opinions. In particular, Gail Napier Johnston, you are a star! I can't thank you enough. *Merci mille fois aussi*, Céline Berthelot.

It's always fun to offer readers an opportunity to be involved in the story. My thanks to Dianne Wallace for contributing the names of the kittens, Bijou and Bonbon. They're perfect!

Congratulations to Alisha Collins, whose name was drawn to contribute the proper names of the fictitious Cooper family who were B&B guests at the Villa. I hope your family enjoys seeing their names on the pages.

The guidance, knowledge and formatting skill of Carolyn Ring has been essential to the publishing of this story.

Many thanks to editor Dinah Forbes for her time, patience and in-depth edit. I always learn so much from her expertise.

The beautiful cover for this book, as for Book One, would not have happened without the talents of artists Clare Strohman and Donna Fedele. The short story of how we started to work together on the covers is that they were on my 2018 south of France tour, that I lead with my good friend Deborah Bine. We got talking about cover art and before we knew it, a very satisfying collaboration had begun.

I'm so grateful to the writing community of which I'm proud to be a part. The collegiality, friendship and support found amongst authors is truly remarkable. Thank you also to the many reviewers and bloggers who take the time to read our novels, review and write about them. I include in my thanks talented designers who create meaningful and beautiful graphics. You all are the lifeline to sharing news about our writing and helping authors expand their readership. The tremendous effort you put into your work is most appreciated.

Special thanks for the assistance of Tonni Callan, Kate

Rock, Sharlene Martin Moore, Barb Drozdowich and Amy Cooper.

And to all the members of the <u>Blue Sky Book Chat group</u> and Patricia's Readers' Rendezvous, *mille mercis* ... a thousand thanks!

My gratitude to every reader who has purchased my work, told others about it, taken the time to write a short review or even written to me. You are the reason I write. I love hearing from you.

ABOUT THE AUTHOR

Canadian author Patricia Sands writes award-winning women's fiction and lives in Toronto, when she isn't somewhere else. Her first novel, *The Bridge Club*, is set in Canada. Her best-selling *Love in Provence* trilogy was drafted in the south of France, where she and her husband spend time each year. *Drawing Lessons*, her fifth novel, researched by Patricia around Arles and the Camargue, was released by Lake Union Publishing on October 1, 2017. *A Season of Surprises at the Villa des Violettes* is the second in a new trilogy of novellas. Patricia often meets with book clubs and women's groups. She leads women's tours to the Côte d'Azur and Provence, based on her novels, and posts articles and photography on popular France-related websites and ezines.

Contact:

Website: www.patriciasandsauthor.com

Amazon Author Page: https://amzn.to/2sJeWrv

Facebook: https:/www.facebook.com/patricia.sands.9

Instagram: https://www.instagram.com/patricialsands/

Blue Sky Book Chat:
   https://www.facebook.com/groups/BlueSkyBookChat/

We hope you enjoy this excerpt from

THE PROMISE OF PROVENCE
(Book I in the LOVE IN PROVENCE Series)

CHAPTER 41

The alarm clock had been set by mutual agreement for Molly's last walk around town before they met Graham and Nick at the daily market in Antibes.

The men were waiting at the appointed spot by the market, drinking coffee and looking undeterred that the women were a little behind schedule.

"Sorry guys, we got caught up in a few stores. I'm into that last chance souvenir shopping panic!"

"No worries! Will you join us for a coffee or should we dive into the *marché*?"

"We're coffee-ed out at the moment. Let's go buy cheese!"

The Monday morning crowd had begun to thin and it was easier to walk up the aisles without the early morning crush.

Nick pointed out the particular stall with a large yellow banner proclaiming Artisan Fromager.

"Oh we bought some cheese there this week," said Katherine.

"Yes, but I happen to know that the guy we're introducing you to was not there this week. He was away. He's the one you need to meet."

Graham was pointing out some of their other favorite stalls when Nick said, "Katherine, I would like to introduce you to the finest cheese expert I have ever known—and thankfully he speaks English!"

Katherine turned around and was stunned.

The man waiting to greet her was none other than Philippe, the nephew of François. Equally stunned, he cocked his head to one side and looked carefully at Katherine, blinking. Nick looked at both of them, wondering what on earth was wrong.

"Katherine?" The answer was like a reflex action. "Katherine! *Quelle surprise*! What are you doing in Antibes?"

"Philippe, I might ask you the same," Katherine said, gasping to catch her breath.

Wiping his hands on his apron, he quickly came around the stand to *bise* her and take her hands.

"*Non*, I live here. This is my shop," he said, waving his arms to take in the entire market. "But you ... you live in Canada."

"It's a long story, but ..." she stumbled over her words, flustered, "I had no idea you lived here. You only mentioned you lived on the coast ... near Nice ..."

They stopped speaking for a moment, looking intently at each other.

"Well, Antibes is where I live," he said, a broad smile spreading across his face.

"I am staying in Antibes for three months and I'm very happy to see you."

"*Oui, moi aussi.*"

Nick watched these exchanges, his head turning from

one to the other as if attending a tennis match. "You know each other, obviously ..."

"Oh Nick, sorry. Yes ... this is so unreal ... Philippe and I met in Provence in June, when I was there for two weeks. We spent some time together ... it's another long story."

The line-up was quickly growing behind Katherine and Nick, with customers beginning to shuffle and mutter with impatience.

Philippe hurried back around to the other side to conduct sales.

"Let's meet for coffee or a drink," Philippe suggested. "I am busy this afternoon, but later today? Say 5 p.m.? The perfect time for a pastis. Nick, come too of course. All of us!"

Katherine hesitated. "I don't know if we will be back by then. We're going to Eze and hiking down the Nietzsche trail this afternoon. I'm not certain how long it will take."

Philippe handed her his card. "Here's my cell. If you aren't there at five, just call me when you do get back. I will keep this evening free. Really, it is incredible to see you here!"

The muttering of irritated voices was becoming noticeable in spite of a co-worker's efforts to pick up the slack. Katherine turned and offered a *désolée* to the people in line. Waving to Philippe, the four hurried off.

Stepping out of the market into the less crowded square, Molly took Katherine by the arm. "That was the Philippe?" she asked, wide eyed. "The gorgeous dude in your photos!"

Katherine nodded, still in shock. Then she briefly told Nick and Graham the story of François and Philippe.

"It's the small world syndrome at play again," Graham commented.

"It's amazing how often that happens!"

"How are you planning to get to Eze?" Nick asked, changing the topic rather abruptly.

"We were reading about it in a guidebook yesterday and can take a train to Villefranche and then the 81 bus up to Eze Village," Katherine said.

Nick chuckled and shook his head. "That bus goes once an hour, and if you miss it, you are out of luck."

"Especially if there's a cruise ship in Villefranche harbor. If the bus is packed, the driver won't even stop for you," interrupted Graham, making a face.

"Do you really want to do that trail?" Nick asked.

Molly nodded enthusiastically. "We have a special connection to Nietzsche going back to when we were kids. We must do it! Right, Kat?"

Kat grinned and nodded. "And Molly is leaving tomorrow, so we have no choice but this afternoon."

"Connection to Nietzsche as kids? That's pretty damn heavy stuff!" Graham said.

Molly laughed. "What doesn't kill us makes us stronger. Katherine's amazing mother gently drilled that into us. It was a message I sure as hell needed in those days."

"When we read about the Nietzsche trail, we knew we had to hike it. We're taking the easy way though—down, not up."

Nick thought for a moment and then offered to drive them up to Eze. "It's not a long drive from here and will take a lot less time than the train and bus. We'll drop you off."

He and Graham exchanged a few words while Molly and Kat agreed with each other that would work nicely.

"Nick that's really kind of you. We don't want to put you out."

"Nah," Graham answered. "In fact you've just given us a

good excuse to roll on into Monte Carlo and play a few hands of poker at the casino. That's our plan."

Nick continued, "Then we can pick you up in Eze-sur-Mer, which is where you will end up. Right by the train station."

He gave her the name of a beach bar just down from the station saying they would wait there and have cold beers on order for their arrival.

"You're going to be ready for a cold brew after that. It's going to be stinkin' hot coming down that cliff. Make sure you take your cell phone, and lots of water. Go get ready and meet us at the boat."

57609590R00135

Made in the USA
Middletown, DE
01 August 2019